W9-BBN-356

Washington Public Library
20 Carlton Avenue
Washington, NJ 07882
(908) 689-0201
www.washboropl.org

Gift
$16.99

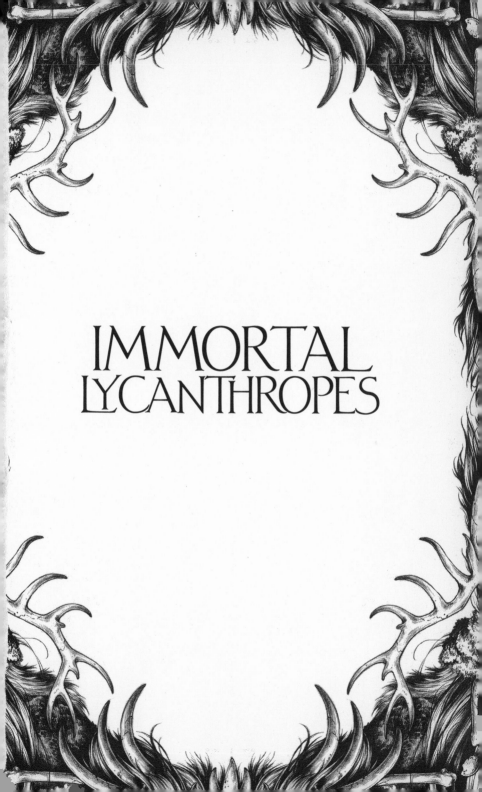

IMMORTAL LYCANTHROPES

IMMORTAL LYCANTHROPES

by Hal Johnson

Illustrations by Teagan White

Clarion Books | Houghton Mifflin Harcourt | Boston New York | 2012

CLARION BOOKS

215 Park Avenue South

New York, New York 10003

Copyright © 2012 by Hal Johnson

Illustrations copyright © 2012 by Teagan White

All rights reserved. For information about permission to reproduce selections from this book,
write to Permissions, Houghton Mifflin Harcourt Publishing Company,
215 Park Avenue South, New York, New York 10003.

Clarion Books is an imprint of
Houghton Mifflin Harcourt Publishing Company.

www.hmhbooks.com

The text was set in Agfa Wile Roman Std.

Book design by Sharismar Rodriguez

Library of Congress Cataloging-in-Publication Data

Johnson, Hal, 1972–

Immortal lycanthropes / by Hal Johnson; with illustrations by Teagan White.

p. cm.

Summary: A young man discovers that he is part of a secret society of immortal were-creatures
bent on hunting one another into extinction.

ISBN 978-0-547-75196-2 (hardcover)

[1. Shapeshifting—Fiction. 2. Supernatural—Fiction.
3. Disfigured persons—Fiction.] I. White, Teagan, ill. II. Title.

PZ7.J63179Im 2012

[Fic]—dc23   2011045438

Manufactured in the United States of America

DOC 10 9 8 7 6 5 4 3 2 1

4500371814

for babsey,

light of my life,

and pinkwater,

fire of my loins

CONTENTS

I

The Derailing

"Perchance," said he, as the five lads lay in the rustling stillness through which sounded the monotonous cooing of the pigeons—"perchance there may be dwarfs and giants and dragons and enchanters and evil knights and whatnot even nowadays. And who knows but that if we Knights of the Rose hold together we may go forth into the world, and do battle with them, and save beautiful ladies, and have tales and gestes written about us as they are writ about the Seven Champions and Arthur his Round-table."

Howard Pyle, *Men of Iron*

I.

A shameful fact about humanity is that some people can be so ugly that no one will be friends with them. It is shameful that humans can be so cruel, and it is shameful that humans can be so ugly.

It would be easy to paint a sob story here, but I am trying to remain objective. So: Myron Horowitz, short, scrawny, and hideous, had no friends. The year before, in eighth grade, he had three people he used to eat lunch with. They had perhaps been his friends, but one had moved away over the summer, one had transferred to a private school, and one had gone through puberty and come out popular. Myron Horowitz had not only not gone through puberty, he had not grown an inch in the last five years, not since his accident. People viewing him from behind assumed he was eight years old; from the front, a different set of assumptions came into play. His face had been partially reconstructed, and it was probably very well done, considering what was left to work with. But it was still a twisted, noseless face, and Myron ate alone now. Worse than eating alone, though, was the walk home. At Henry Clay High School, students who took a bus home passed from their locker through the gymnasium to convene in the parking lot; students who walked home took a different route, through the cafeteria and out through a side door, along a wooded path to the sidewalk. Very few students walked home, but Myron did, and so did Garrett Bercelli.

Garrett was not overly large for a freshman, but compared to Myron he was a heavyweight champion. His hands especially were large, and, as they say, sinewy. He probably had reasons for his antisocial behavior, but, frankly, they don't concern me. He can die and go to hell for all I care, once he has served his purpose in our narrative.

There are disadvantages, I am aware, to beginning our story this fast. Perhaps I should have given Myron a few scenes at home, curled up with his adventure books or bumping elbows with his parents at their cozy breakfast nook. But really, who wants to see that horrible face eat? And anyway, we have places to go. Myron, two years ago, had had a fourth friend, but he died; that part is pretty funny, when you think about it, and if you are heartless, but I barely have time to mention Danny Fitzsimmons. We have places to go. People will turn into animals, and here come ancient secrets and rivers of blood.

It was on a crisp October day in suburban western Pennsylvania, beneath the golden panoply of leaves some people find so charming, that Garrett Bercelli introduced himself to Myron by picking him up and playfully throwing him into a pricker bush. Two days later he cut right to the chase and punched Myron in the stomach. That was a Friday. On Monday, Garrett really went wild; he forbore (so he explained during the course of the beating) to touch Myron's horrible face, but he pummeled the rest of his body quite mercilessly. At last Myron spat up some blood, and Garrett ran away.

Obviously I cannot literally enter Garrett Bercelli's head, to observe the shadow parade of his thought processes, but I have investigated the matter enough that I believe I can produce a fairly accurate reconstruction. Garrett ran home, convinced, I believe, that he had killed or maimed poor Myron. This fact in itself did not concern him, but the risk that he would be caught, and punished, was enough to send him hiding in his bed, the way he had as a child. He hadn't meant to kill Myron, after all, and this should be taken into account. It had all been juvenile high spirits, and things had just gone too far. Garrett could hardly remember the beating, he could just remember the feeling it had given him, the rushing sound in his ears and the reckless abandon. Whether it gave him an erection I do not pretend to know, but let's assume the answer is yes. The idea that anything as wonderful as the emotions he had undergone in the course of that afternoon could land him in the reformatory was intolerable. He went to school the next day filled with righteous indignation and a healthy dollop of fear (he had, in fact, tried to feign sickness, but his mother would have none of it). Imagine his relief when he saw, in homeroom, Myron at his desk, alive and apparently hale. The relief would have quickly turned to excitement. You may recall the feeling you have had on first discovering that the author of a favorite book had written a dozen more, perhaps under various pseudonyms, the feeling of a world of possibilities opening up. Garrett did not know what that felt like, because, as best I have been able to determine, he had never finished a book not assigned to school, and few of those. As I said, he probably had reasons for being so violent, reasons that do not concern us. But what Garrett felt at that moment was analogous to a reader's joy. Here was something he could do, something he was good at and could get away with.

"Tuesday, fish sticks; Wednesday, spaghetti; Thursday, meat loaf . . ." the loudspeaker was intoning for the week, when Garrett leaned down a half inch from Myron's ear.

"If you miss one day," he hissed, referring either to school or to their meetings after and behind it, "I will kill you."

Myron was less pleased with the arrangement. His entire body still ached from yesterday's pummeling, obviously, and there had been blood in his urine. He considered telling his parents, his adoptive parents who had taken him in after the accident. Dr. and Mrs. Horowitz were good people—you don't adopt a deformed eight-year-old unless you are reasonably unselfish—but it's no use pretending they understood him. They made a game effort, but a child who never grew an inch from the moment he had been found crawling dazed and torn up along the Maine coast five years ago never really made much sense to them. When Myron looked upset (for example), they cheerfully tended to remind him that at his next birthday he'd be allowed a cell phone, unaware that his true worry was that he'd have no one to call. They were always unaware. I don't want to have a pity party for Myron Horowitz. He ends up okay, and I have frankly had worse days than his that week. But I have not had many days worse than his worst. Myron was scared, and he was too scared to admit to anyone that he was scared. He had thought about carrying a knife, and had even packed one to bring to school that day, a steak knife from his mother's kitchen, but it fell out of his knapsack somewhere between home and school, which may have been for the best. Tuesday was a long, slow day; every day at school is a long, slow day, but this one was something special.

That Tuesday afternoon, after school, Myron decided to try leaving by a different route. From his locker he slipped downstairs and into the lobby, the one with the trophy cases and the door to the administrative offices. If he could go out the school's wide front door, he would be on a busy street, where Garrett would, presumably, be unable to make his assault. Myron may have been a little afraid that Garrett would make good his threat, his threat to kill him, but he was absolutely terrified of another beating like yesterday's. He knew it would be shameful to cry, but he was afraid enough that he could feel the tears welling. He was often called "Baby" by his peers, just because of his height, and he was desperate not to have the nickname lengthened to "Crybaby." "Chip" was the nickname he had selected for himself and that no one used. Garrett's nickname for him, which was catching on around the school, was "Faggot."

As Myron approached the front doors, he heard a voice behind him, saying, "Young man"—the vice principal's voice, he realized, as he turned around.

Myron said nothing in response.

"Where do you think you're going?" asked the vice principal, a Mr. Zaborsky, famous at the country club, perhaps, for his slice, but known at Henry Clay primarily for having hair in his ears and a butt crack that peeked over his belt like a mischievous gremlin when he was standing up, only to leap forth with a yawning maw if God forbid he should bend over. This is all terribly unfair to the man, but Myron was so terrifyingly ugly that it is sometimes necessary to remind those of his acquaintance that ugliness is all around, and not limited to that hideous face. Right now, in fact, there is something ugly happening under a rock nearby; if you are near a rock, turn it over and you will see a worm going to the bathroom. Ugly things are happening in your intestines as you read this. A million million ugly microbes are crawling on your skin. Have you even been in a dim room and seen, in the one ray of light that lanced some distance away through the window, a sparkling miasma of dust motes? And have you then thought to yourself, *Thank the good Lord I am not on that side of the room, in that sunbeam,—for if I were, every breath would require the inhalation of that furry, filthy air?* It's just as dusty where you're standing, of course, but you are able to pretend it is not. That's the kind of deception you're apt to put over on yourself when you see Myron. Perhaps that was what Mr. Zaborsky was thinking as he wiggled his hips and tugged at his pants.

"Home?" Myron asked.

"Home? Home? Don't you know," Mr. Zaborsky intoned, rather enjoying the moment, "that all those not taking a bus are to exit through the cafeteria?"

"I didn't think it would matter," Myron said, in a very quiet voice. "This way is closer for me, is all."

"Closer for you?" Mr. Zaborsky rather began to strut. He hooked his thumbs in imaginary suspenders. It is likely that in his mind he was a great orator, and he only on occasion had the opportunity to employ the art that was his secret calling. "The exit to which you are headed is reserved for faculty, staff, and visitors. Students are privileged with their own twin exits, one through the gymnasium and one through the cafeteria. Now, what would happen if we all decided to ignore the rules, and just go our own merry way? Anarchy, that's what! Do you know what anarchy is?"

With infinite patience, and, doubtless, not without kindness and wisdom, Mr. Zaborsky perorated about the benefits of a law and the pandemonium of lawlessness. When he finally watched Myron turn and trudge back to the cafeteria, he beamed with the saintly face of someone who has "made a difference." But don't be too hard on him. It is no easy thing, never to have made a difference; and, to be fair, when he heard the news the next morning, he momentarily wondered if he could have done anything to prevent it. Quickly he concluded that he had done all that was humanly possible, but he did have that moment, and that moment is something.

Nervously, to himself, Myron hummed as he entered the cafeteria.

You have perhaps already anticipated that Garrett Bercelli, tiring of the wait, unaware that his date had been held captive by Zaborsky's endless lecture, had been himself drawn into the cafeteria, where he was standing, awkwardly, when Myron entered.

The cafeteria was a foolish place to try anything, because, although the room was empty now, the internal wall facing the hallway was nothing but a row of large windows. Across the hall were the windows of the nurse's office, and the nurse always stayed late; she could easily see anything untoward happening in the cafeteria, if she just looked over. But Garrett was too excited to waste time dragging his prey outside.

"You know you're going to have to pay for making me wait," he said. He was smiling as he said it, and it was a genuine smile. He was so happy, his hands were shaking.

"Leave me alone," said Myron unconvincingly. He was a very tiny boy, I hope I have stressed, as well as an ugly one.

"What happened to your face, anyway, faggot?"

"I don't remember," Myron said, which was true. He remembered nothing of the accident, nor of his life before it.

"I'm going to give you something to remember."

After that some other things happened, and then there was a loud crashing sound. The nurse, and then several teachers, came running. (Mr. Zaborsky was in the bathroom.)

As a safety precaution, the school had some years before begun installing shatterproof glass, the kind with hexagons of chicken wire inside it. Then new safety advisories had indicated that the chicken-wire glass was in fact more dangerous than regular glass, for reasons that should become clear soon, and the school had stopped the replacements; but it had never gotten around to undoing what it had done.

This bit of history, dug up and reported in the local papers that week, is necessary for an understanding of how it was that Garrett smashed through the regular windows between the cafeteria and the hallway, and smashed into the reinforced shatterproof windows of the nurse's office. He became caught in the chicken wire, several feet off the ground, and hung there, bleeding.

And there in the cafeteria—it was weird. All the tables and chairs, all of them, were tipped over and scattered to the periphery of the room. And alone in the center lay Myron, unconscious and totally naked.

They never found more than a few strips of his clothes, although the air was filled with wisps of cotton and loose, tumbling threads.

2.

Mystery explosion rocks Westfield high school, everybody said. The explosion wasn't what caught on, though. It was the mystery. What kind of explosion could propel one student through a window, blow all the clothes off another, and scatter chairs and tables without even damaging, some scuff marks excepted, the floor? Henry Clay High School, Westfield, Pennsylvania, had a genuine unexplained phenomenon.

The school nurse got to Myron first. She hadn't even seen Garrett, who was, after all, several feet off the ground and partly obscured by chicken wire and broken glass. She ran to Myron, covered him with her shawl, and ran back to her office to call the police, who had already been called by others. When she returned, Myron was surrounded by teachers. "Give him air," she shrieked, not sure what else to do. She then ran back to her office, saw Garrett stuck in her window, and fell over. When the ambulance came, it took Myron and a hyperventilating nurse (Mrs. Botchel, the newspaper said) to the hospital. Garrett, now awake and screaming, had to be cut out of the chicken wire, and required a second trip. This is why reinforced windows are dangerous, incidentally.

Myron had no memory of what had happened. His attempts to explain are perhaps worth recording, if only in paraphrase. He had felt a pressure, and he had felt a lack of pressure, and then he was aware of looking at two opposite sides of the room at once, and then everything had gone dark. He was covered in bruises, dismissed as superficial because they faded quickly. Nothing else was wrong with him, and the police, although puzzled, could hardly pin a trashed cafeteria on one scrawny kid. So after an overnight (for observation), Myron was free to go. He had made quite a hit that night among the hospital staff, who were compassionate people desensitized from their internships in the burn ward and pitied the ugly little boy; they took turns showing him around, and his happiest moments came when touring the newborn ward. He had to wear a surgeon's cap and mask, and no infant screamed when it saw him.

The Horowitzes, on hospital orders, told their son that he should take it easy, and, at the sheriff's suggestion, encouraged him to try to remember what the devil had happened. He was out of school for a week. (Garrett, in case you care, which I don't, recovered almost completely, but began wetting the bed compulsively; perhaps he'll recover his dignity in time. He also remembered nothing, or said he remembered nothing, after a certain point. "I heard air rushing, and I was looking at the dark," was all he could say.) Myron spent his week reading adventure novels on the couch, and eating cookies.

Most of this information was in the local news, accompanied by wildly inaccurate speculations about an explosion. Everyone assumed, of course, that Myron and Garrett had just been walking amiably by, innocent bystanders to some kind of occult phenomenon. The mystery was a slim sidebar in a couple of national papers, which was where I read about it. So I packed up an overnight bag, a gun, a thermos, and an extra can of gas, and I called Alice.

At his parents' request, Myron's return to school was a quiet affair. "Let's act as though nothing happened," they may as well have painted on a bedsheet banner and hung in the front hall. Lunch tables the custodian moved to the gymnasium temporarily. In the lunchroom, workmen got paint on their coveralls.

If I may be permitted a moment of melodrama (which is after all the idiom of my chosen profession), there were two smoke-filled basements in which Myron's return to school caught a sinister eye. One of them was in Baton Rouge. The other was in Westfield, Pennsylvania. Unlike Myron, Garrett Bercelli was not without friends. Three or four of them had gone to visit ol' Garrett in his hospital bed; had heard his secret whisper that Horowitz had, somehow (he remembered nothing!), done this to him; had later in a metaphorically smoke-filled basement made a secret pact to find Myron Horowitz after school and 1. steal his backpack; 2. remove, and 2a. steal, his pants; and 3. "teach him a lesson" through violence. Violence was their idiom. Perhaps it was not yet, but it would be before long, and they were testing the waters on a small, ugly boy, who would soon be, they high-fived each other in celebratory anticipation, bloody and half-naked. It would be pretty funny, you must admit, if you are heartless.

Donald Chang, Michael West, and one or two others needed time to make their clever plans. And so it was three days later that they lay in wait for Myron Horowitz, who was, incidentally, no happier, and no handsomer, than he had been before this whole foofarah. It never rains but it pours, they say; they say a lot of things. Myron was walking down the street. Was he whistling to himself? Was he dreaming of a brighter future not to be his?

Westfield is a pleasant, small, suburban community. There are almost no sidewalks. The front lawns are large, trees scant, and there is, consequently, a dearth of places to hide in ambush. But this was why our conspirators (Donald, etc.) had waited for this day. This was Thursday, and Thursday was garbage day; large, green, plastic, identical garbage cans sat at the end of every driveway. They had already been emptied of their garbage. Our conspirators (West, etc.) had, that day, run ahead of Myron as he walked home from school—students were allowed to use the front exit now, until the lunchroom paint dried—run to the end of Myron's block, and secreted themselves, one each, beneath the hinged lid of a trash can. Three or four garbage cans total. It had rained earlier, and at the bottom of each can sat a quarter inch of stagnant garbage water. The stench was formidable. But it would all be worth it for the money shot, when out of three or four garbage cans leapt three or four bringers of the mayhem.

Please note that I am not being cute here. I have been unable to ascertain the exact number of mayhem bringers.

Myron's house, or rather his parents' house, was scarcely visible down the block, a good hundred yards away from the site of ambush. Perhaps he saw a garbage can lid twitch, for young Myron suddenly stopped whistling, then stopped walking altogether. From scant trees' leaves dripped the remains of the morning rainfall. The road was black and shiny still. Myron was not quite at the spot he was supposed to have reached, but what, thought everyone, the hell. First one, and then another sprang from the garbage cans in a way they had probably discussed. Such springing is, in fact, very difficult to do, and in every case the can tipped over, spilling out a wet and filthy boy who was standing up, dusting himself off, and thirsting for blood.

"Take off your pants," one said, prematurely. There was supposed to be an order to these things.

Myron tensed. If he had started running when the cans commenced falling over, he probably could have gotten away, but, frankly, he had not expected to be assaulted here, or in this fashion. He may have expected from a garbage can to have emerged a raccoon, and true raccoons can be pleasant company. Now it was too late to run, he was surrounded by people with longer legs; now he was ready to sprint at any opportunity, now that there was no opportunity forthcoming.

From up ahead, near Myron's house, a station wagon pulled out from the curb. Of course, no one noticed it.

"What did you do to Garrett?" one person was inquiring, while another was suggesting that Myron might want to drop his backpack and make this easier. Perhaps these two speaking were Donald Chan and Michael West. Both were killed, one quickly and one slowly over the course of six futile surgical procedures, after the speeding station wagon struck them. This happened very quickly, and to call it a surprise would probably be understating things, especially for Messrs. Chan and West. But this was also Myron's opportunity, and he had already begun sprinting, sideways, across the lawn, not toward his house but simply away. God help him, he was glad the car had struck; knowing him, as I do now, he probably did not think his classmates were dead; or perhaps he was too scared to care. Across the generous front lawn and across the generous back lawn he ran, and as he ran, and his mind processed what had happened, he gradually became less scared of the small cadre of bullies and more scared of a station wagon and its homicide of a driver. Soon Myron was on the front lawn of another street, Pennylane Place, if I recall correctly. He saw, to his right, rounding the corner, a station wagon with blood on its hood. A thin woman with short blond hair and sunglasses, he could dimly perceive, was behind the wheel. She could not follow him across the lawns, of course, but her car was much faster than he, and, houses being spaced out as they were, Myron had nowhere to hide. He turned around, ready to run back, and he saw a man there, huge and wild-haired and dressed, unseasonably, in a long leather duster. His nose was as long and square and thin as an ax blade. His back was hunched; patches of long black hairs tufted his chin. The man looked terrifying, for all sorts of objective reasons, but he also made the hairs on Myron's neck stand up, in a way nothing else ever had. There was a shadow of a memory he could not articulate associated with this sensation. What with all that, it took Myron a moment to realize that the man, whoever he was, had been in the station wagon and had gotten out to chase him.

"What are you?" the man said.

Myron stood paralyzed. He had hardly led a life that had prepared him for acts of violence beyond schoolyard bullying, pummeling and pantslessness, and a little bit of blood. Driving through two people, killing two people—

(One or two people got away. Minors, their names were kept out of the papers if they were ever learned at all.)

—this was another order of cruelty, to which the Garretts of this world, and their friends, could only aspire in time.

The station wagon, behind him, had parked, and Myron could hear the door opening. He risked a quick glance behind and quickly took in a tall, pale woman striding across the lawn toward him. In front of him, "You're the kid who fought the lion and mane?" the man said, and took a step forward. The afternoon sun was behind the stranger, and he was close enough now that his shadow touched Myron's shoe.

Just then a pickup truck jumped the curb, skidded across the lawn, and churned to a halt in between Myron and his interlocutor. The passenger side window was down, and from within a smartly dressed young woman, her long black hair in a ponytail, said, "Hop in the back, this is a rescue."

That was Alice saying that. But I was behind the wheel.

3.

There is a cacophony inside my mouth. I have read a lot of books in my life, and have written more than a few, and, if not all of them, then at least many of them are still there in my mouth in one way or another.

I mean, there are, of course, many ways of telling a story. Horace recommends starting in the middle; the King of Hearts recommends starting at the beginning. Obviously Myron's story started a while ago, with the accident and all, but I didn't start back there. Why should you know more than Myron did?

I lived with the Ainu of northern Japan, once, some time ago, and there I encountered an epic poem collected and published under the name "Repunnotunkur" that ran for some five hundred lines of adventures for the narrator, before that narrator was asked to give an account, to a curious man, of everything that had happened thus far—and the poem just repeats it, word for word, five hundred lines, up to the present moment.

Readers would probably not have the patience to let a narrative start over. Imagine if, three chapters from now, Myron Horowitz were asked how he got here, and he replied, "A shameful fact about humanity . . ." I'd certainly close the book.

Oh, we asked him how he got here, and he didn't answer. He just looked dumbly at us. He was kneeling in the flatbed of the truck as we raced through the sidestreets. It might have been a little scary for a kid.

A small window separated the flatbed from the cab of the truck. Alice slid the window open. "What's your name?" she asked.

He told us.

"Jeez Louise, you got screwed, kid," I said. "Look, what's going on? Why is Benson after you? And where'd you come from, for that matter?"

"What are you talking about? How would I know what's going on? I don't know who Benson is. I don't know how you fight a lion and its mane. I don't know who you are or where you're taking me."

"Hey, don't cry, Myron," Alice said. He was crying. "My name is Alice, and this is my friend Arthur."

"That's me!" I said.

"Benson was the big guy who was chasing you. His driver was Mignon Emanuel. They work for Mr. Bigshot. Does that help?"

"I have no idea what you're even talking about. Are you police?"

"Oh, lawsy, no," Alice said. "We're, you know, like you."

"Like me?"

"We're lycanthropes."

"We're what?"

"Technically," I pointed out helpfully, for I abhor imprecision, "we are therianthropes."

"You're werewolves?" Myron asked.

"No, no, I was just saying, and this is why I abhor imprecision," I said, "lycanthropes are werewolves, and we certainly do not turn into wolves."

"I was using *lycanthrope* colloquially," Alice insisted. "I didn't mean wolves, I meant were-animals."

"You're crazy," Myron said. He had stopped crying at least, but he looked like he was going to go all hysterical at any moment.

"We saved your life," Alice said, "crazy or not. And we can turn into animals."

As we pulled onto the highway our truck hit a bump that threw Myron against the window. I'd been watching him in the rearview mirror, and when his face came up to the window, I gave a start. He was really ugly. The features weren't even in the right place was the problem. One eye was lower than the other, and the bridge of his nose was shaped like a seven, and it ended in nothing. Myron drew his face away from the window, pulled off his backpack, and sat on it. The flatbed must have been wet, come to think. "What animals?" he asked.

"I'm a red panda, and Arthur's a binturong."

"What's a binturong?" Myron asked.

I was getting annoyed. "It's a bearcat. What, like you're something cooler?"

"You turn into a bearcat?"

"No, Myron, he is a bearcat. He's a bearcat who turns into a human."

I growled, "Can we just say *binturong?* I'm a binturong. A binturong is driving your car. You're going to have to learn the word eventually."

Alice was still calm, damn her eyes. "What are you, Myron?"

"I'm . . . I'm Jewish?"

"No, I mean, what animal. What do you turn into a human from?"

"I don't turn from anything into anything. This is crazy, you don't turn into anything, either."

"Show him," Alice said.

"I can't, I'm driving."

She grabbed the wheel and swung a foot over onto the gas pedal. "You can, I can't—I'm wearing the wrong kind of clothes." And she was right, her clothes were for street wear, it would've taken her forever to put them back on. Whereas

I was dressed stylishly but sensibly, so I turned into a binturong. Shaggy black fur, tufts on the tops of my ears, and a long, sinuous tail. I popped back into human form right away, and now I was naked, of course, my clothes strewn about the font seat where they had fallen.

"You can change form, too," Alice said, relinquishing the wheel and dropping a shirt in my lap, for modesty's sake. "Do you not know what you are?"

"Because we sure don't know," I said, "so don't look to us for the answer. Also, it's cold in here, close the window."

Alice did not close the window between us and Myron, of course, which I suppose made sense. The kid took this all pretty well, considering, and said, "Maybe, maybe I just haven't turned into anything yet. Maybe at puberty I'll start turning into something, at the full moon."

"Jeez Louise, kid, not that old full-moon bromide. And I've got bad news for you: you're never going to hit puberty."

"Are you going to kill me?"

I was so frustrated that I leaned forward and bit the steering wheel. He was so slow to catch on!

"We saved your life," Alice said, "we'd hardly kill you now. You're safe, we're just trying to figure things out."

"How do you know I can turn into something?"

"We can feel it, when we're around one of our own kind. Can you get the feeling from us?"

"Yeah, like your neck's all prickly. I got the same feeling from the big guy."

"Benson. He's one of us, too. He's a bison."

"That's how he got his name," I added helpfully.

"And Mignon Emanuel, the woman driving the car, and Mr. Bigshot—they're like us, too."

Myron said, "Benson looked like an Indian, an American Indian."

"Of course he did, where do you think bison are from?" Alice said. "I'm from Burma, or it's Myanmar now. Arthur's from Indochina, probably around Cambodia. It's hard to tell where you're from."

"With a map like that," I muttered. By *map* I meant *pan*—I meant his face.

"Why won't I hit puberty?" Myron said. You couldn't distract him from the important stuff.

I said, "You haven't hit puberty yet, have you? And everyone else you knew did, I bet."

"The doctor said I was slow to develop."

Alice said, "I don't know how you can't know this stuff. Surely you've noticed that you don't age. You're stuck at that age, just like I'll be twenty-three and Arthur will be seventeen forever."

"I'm more like twenty, twenty-one really," I said.

"Forever?" Myron said.

"Of course, you fool! Haven't you noticed?" I was squirming all over my seat, I couldn't stand it. Also, I was cold. "You're immortal."

"I can't be immortal, I'm only thirteen years old!"

"You can't be thirteen years old, you're immortal." I felt

something like an itch inside my nose, but I chalked it up to nerves. "The only thing that can kill you is one of us. In animal form. With the claws and the teeth."

"You could kill me?"

"Well, probably not, I'm a binturong. We're pretty harmless. But for all I know, you could be a vole. I could kill a vole."

"What's a vole?"

"Like a field mouse, stop asking quest—"

But Alice interrupted me. "Someone's nearby."

And they came up the ramp, onto the highway, the station wagon with Mignon Emanuel and Benson. I floored it and they floored it, and I said, "How did they find us?"

"They must've known we were going to see Gloria," Alice said. Her head was turned around, her eyes glued on the station wagon as it slowly gained on us.

"How could they possibly know that?"

"She's in Shoreditch, that's pretty close to here."

"Who's Gloria?" Myron asked. But just then there was a loud, sharp noise, and he cried, "They're shooting at me!"

"They're not shooting at you," I replied, with calm assurance and nerves of steel. "They're shooting at the tires."

"What, so they don't want to kill me?"

I checked the rearview. Benson had his arm out the window, carelessly blasting away with a pistol. With his other hand he was attempting to manipulate a CB radio. What an idiot. I considered telling Alice to get my own pistol from the glove compartment, but I didn't want her to end up looking as stupid as Benson did. Instead, I said to Myron, "Anyone wants to kill you, I told you, bullets won't do the job."

"So they *do* want to kill me?"

"How the devil would I know? Jeez Louise, kid, I'm driving here. Now hold on, I'm going to try something tricky."

I yanked the wheel left, crashed over the median, skidded backwards on the wet road, whipped around, bounced in a shower of sparks off a stone embankment, and drove the wrong way under a bridge and down an on-ramp. We threaded around a descending railroad gate, made a U-turn that involved at least two people's lawns, and cut through a city park to avoid a red light. Alice screamed and laughed, and, frankly, I was screaming and laughing, too. I was impressed with the kid, that he never made a peep. Fifteen minutes later, after a half-dozen other moving violations, we pulled into a gas station, and noticed that Myron Horowitz was no longer in the flatbed.

"I told him to hold on," I said, but Alice put her hand on my arm and shut me up. Inside his backpack, which he had left behind, was a book I had written sixty years ago.

II

The Derailing

PART TWO

As for me, it was only by thinking how the late Baron Trenck would have conducted himself under similar circumstances that I was able to restrain my tears.

Thomas Bailey Aldrich, *The Story of a Bad Boy*

I.

Myron Horowitz regained consciousness in a soggy ditch. Two black children were looking down at him and speaking French. He was in so much pain he passed out again. When he came back, he was on a couch, wrapped in a blanket. A very broad man was looking down at him.

"What did they tell you?" the man asked.

"They told me I was an immortal lycanthrope," Myron said.

"You're in shock—drink this," the man said. Myron drank it and passed out.

It would be tedious to enumerate the number of times he came into and out of consciousness. "I've been hurt worse," Myron insisted, and that was certainly true, but he couldn't remember that hurt, and that made all the difference. Children, all younger than Myron, although not younger than he looked, would come down a flight of stairs bearing orange juice and aspirin. Sometimes they would bring just the aspirin, along with an empty glass and a guilty look. The walls of the room were wood-paneled, and the carpet was a thick dark red, and filthy. A bedpan was utilized, for the first day at least—but Myron had trouble keeping track of time. Occasionally the sound of a distant train would whistle through the windowless walls. At last the broad man returned. He was wearing a tattered robe and leafed through the mail as he walked. The mail went into a pocket in the robe as he sat on an ottoman.

"I thought you were worse off than you were. It was your face, see. That's all old wounds, I guess, but it had so much dirt on it, I thought it just got tore off."

"No, it's old," Myron conceded.

"You was bleeding some, and I thought your legs was broke, but I guess not. I guess you're going to be okay, with a headache maybe. You was talking crazy for a while."

"I do have a headache. Can I call my parents? I've had kind of a weird time of it, and they must be worried."

"Sure, you can call your parents, but after we talk. We've got to talk first, see." The man reached down, groped under the couch, came up with a cigarette butt, and lit it with a transparent lighter. "My name is Mr. Rodriguez, and I run a kind of school here for international students. You may have noticed the many international young people running around."

"It's very impressive," Myron said.

"They are students, of course, and I run a kind of school. I can show you my papers, papers from the government that show I have a school."

"It sounds like a delightful school."

Mr. Rodriguez looked at Myron a long time in silence. "How old are you, now, eight?"

"Thirteen, actually."

"Well, I prescribe plenty of bed rest and some fruit juice. You're healing nice. Kids heal real fast with bed rest and fruit juice."

"Maybe I can call my parents now?"

"We don't got no phone. Schools are for learning, not foolery, so of course we got no phone. But I'll send Kwame to the candy store, have him call. Write your number down here." Mr. Rodriguez groped around, looking for a pen, finally located one behind his ear, and then groped around for a piece of paper. He settled on a torn-open envelope, part of the day's mail. Myron neatly printed out his number and passed the envelope back. Mr. Rodriguez turned away.

"My name," Myron called after him.

"Your what?"

"My name. You should tell my parents my name."

"Right. What is it, then?"

"Myron."

Without a word, Mr. Rodriguez nodded and left. From his fist, Myron removed the wadded-up paper he had slid from the envelope.

He was excited to have acquired a clue, like a character from one of the adventure books he liked to read. "I'll figure out what's going on here," he muttered.

"Hello," said a voice, and Myron jumped. The ball of paper fell from his hand. A young Asian boy bearing a glass stepped forward and picked it up.

"You are Myron," the boy said. "I am John."

"Did you bring me fruit juice?" Myron guessed.

"I think water." He passed over the glass and the paper.

"Do you know what kind of school this is?" Myron asked.

"We learn very good English," John said.

"Where are you from, John?"

"I am Malay. We learn very good. Mr. Rodriguez is good man." His eyes looked terrified.

"Where is a Malay from?"

"Malaysia. In Indochina."

"Have you ever seen a binturong?"

"A binturong?"

"Um. A bearcat? Black and shaggy, long tail." He gestured with his hands.

"Ah, binturong. Very nice, very pretty."

"Do you trust binturongs?" Myron asked, but of course John said nothing. It was a stupid question.

Myron drank the water and passed the glass back. John left. Holding his breath and listening for anyone to arrive, Myron quickly unwadded the paper. "You may already have won . . ." it said. Some clue! Myron tossed it to the ground angrily, where it bounced back off the ottoman and rolled under the couch.

From the top of the stairs came John's whisper. "We are all prison."

2.

"It's like this, Kwame," Myron said. "I've read a lot of books about people wandering into strange or frightening situations, and what kind of things they can do. If the situation was different I wouldn't mind hanging around to find out what was going on and then, you know, freeing everyone. But a few days ago a man and a woman tried to kill me, with a car and with a gun. Another man and woman saved my life, and they told me I was an immortal lycanthrope, although I don't turn into a wolf. Well, really they don't know what I turn into. And I fell out of a speeding car and I didn't die, so maybe they're right. But I've got to get out of here and find out if I'm really a werewolf or what, so I'm not going to stay, I'm sorry. But before I go, I need to know what town this is. Do you know what town this is? Where we live?" He tried it several times, at slower speeds, but Kwame couldn't understand him. Kwame spoke a language Myron had never heard before, from somewhere in western Africa. He also spoke French.

It was in French that Kwame spoke to Jack (not his real name; Mr. Rodriguez had given it to him), an Algerian, and also Binky (not his real name; Mr. Rodriguez had given it to him), Vietnamese. Binky had become friends with Lord Thundercheese (not his real name; Mr. Rodriguez had given it to him), Nigerian, and had worked out a kind of private pidgin between the two. Bancroft (not his real name; Mr. Rodriguez had given it to him), Sudanese, could speak Arabic with Jack, as well as English with our friend John (not his real name; Mr. Rodriguez had given it to him). There were several other kids running around—at least one from Russia and one from a temporary autonomous zone that no nation but Cuba had ever recognized as sovereign—but Myron hadn't figured out how they all fit in.

For that matter, Kwame was not his real name. Mr. Rodriguez had given it to him. He was from Senegal.

The English speakers at odd hours explained in whispers what Myron had already concluded: that Mr. Rodriguez did not, in fact, run a school for international students. He collected an assortment of fees, some from a guardian or government official, and some from nonprofit groups that sponsored the students. The children spent the day eating very little and on occasion laboriously copying sample letters Rodriguez had penned and that most of them couldn't read. These letters extolled their ongoing education, and asked for spending money.

"If I could figure out where we are, I could sneak to a phone and call my parents."

"No phone here," John pointed out.

Mr. Rodriguez spent a lot of time elsewhere, sometimes coming home very late, and usually soused and angry. Sometimes, while he was gone, the kids were locked in the house; sometimes they were locked out, but Myron was always locked in.

"Just go to the police while you're out," Myron begged, but Bancroft shook his head in fear.

"American police make AIDS."

The international students would, as a rule, rather spend their time foraging for food. They hated but respected Mr. Rodriguez, and they trusted absolutely no one else, including Myron.

"Just ask them what town we're in, Bancroft. I need to know how far from Westfield we are."

Bancroft demurred. The inhabitants of this strange land were not to be trusted.

Mr. Rodriguez ignored most of his charges, but he looked at Myron suspiciously. The doors, of course, were deadbolted. There were bars on the first-story windows.

During the days, and nights, that Mr. Rodriguez was gone, Myron wandered the house, at first looking for a way out, then seeking a clue to his current location, and finally just poking his nose around. In a drawer were several bundles of pamphlets for Featherstone Academy, "an elite multicultural educational setting in beautiful Pennsylvania, USA," with crudely retouched photographs of Tudor houses and acres of rolling grasslands; but the place where the return address sticker would go was blank. He found quite a stash of pornographic magazines, too, but they were, on the one hand, too tailored to bizarre niche tastes and, on the other hand, too overt a reminder that Myron had still not hit puberty for him to enjoy.

"I sure feel older, though," he said to himself, and waited for his growth spurt. He hummed happily. He was, after all, having an adventure.

Mr. Rodriguez's house had two floors in addition to the finished basement. Most of the rooms were given over to sleeping quarters for the innumerable students. Either Mr. Rodriguez was a man of surprising discrimination and taste, or whoever had lived here before him had left some stuff behind. The crumbling bookshelves held three nonconsecutive volumes of Macaulay's *Critical and Historical Essays,* and several Kafka paperbacks. On one wall, in the stairwell, hung a dusty old picture Myron recognized, by Degas. His parents had owned a poster reproduction of the painting; it was a famous painting, Myron knew, and he wondered if Mr. Rodriguez knew how much this picture was worth, and what a fortune he had here.

"Fortune!" Myron shouted, and ran down two flights to the basement. He dug under the couch. Here he found half a dozen cigarette fragments and a crumpled piece of paper, which held forth the promise of riches to a certain:

Andre Rodriguez
17 Lightning Hill Rd.
Picthatch, PA

Myron knew where Picthatch was! Not fifteen miles from Westfield. He thought for a while about clever ways to sneak out of the house, and he even tried to go up the chimney. Finally he threw a chair through a second-story window (the latch had rusted shut). He looked down a dizzying height.

"What you doing there?" shouted up John, who was wandering by outside. In his hand he had a noose he had braided out of floss, with which he hoped to catch chipmunks for dinner.

"If I am truly immortal, I could just jump," Myron whispered. But instead, he dragged a bedroll to the window and, after a great deal of straining, managed to wedge it through. Once free, it unfurled and fell to the grass below.

"Hey!" John shouted. "Not use mine!"

One by one, five more bedrolls tumbled through, followed by some couch cushions, until they made a nice pile. Myron carefully checked the window frame for broken glass, stuck his feet through, and—he held his breath but did not close his eyes—slithered through into the air. When he landed on the soft pile, a great cloud of dust erupted, hiding him from sight. By the time it cleared, he was already running across the trash-strewn lawn.

"I'm escaping!" he shouted. "Anyone who wants to can come with me."

The boys whistled and whooped, but they did not follow him. He passed a copse of birch trees, a collection of rusting fragmented automobiles, etc. Clouds rushed by overhead. The air felt heavy. It was the first time he'd been outside since he he'd arrived here. He was still wearing the same muddy clothes, and his underwear had grown strange and crispy. How many weeks had it been? In the distance, he could hear, and then see, the passing train. The air was cold enough to show his breath, like a smokestack.

A deep, wide ditch separated the tracks from the field, and Myron, out of breath, walked along the outside rim of the ditch, following the tracks. When he finally came to a place where the tracks crossed a road, he thought he recognized where he had fallen from our pickup. Myron followed the road a ways until he came to a small collection of stores. In front of a laundromat, a bald, tired man was sitting on a milk crate.

"Is there a phone around here?" Myron asked.

"Inside, costs a dime."

Myron had prepared for this as he walked along the tracks. He presented to the man two beer bottles he had picked up on the way. "Can I trade you?" he asked.

With his newly acquired dime, he called his parents. "I'm in Picthatch, you won't believe it, come get me," he couldn't help crowing. Things had gotten exciting, and it really felt, now, like an adventure.

The voice on the other end was muffled. "Where in Pic-thatch are you exactly?" It was a strange voice.

"Who is this?" Myron asked.

"This is Mrs. Wangenstein, your guidance counselor. Am I remembered by you, Myron?"

"What are you doing there?"

"I was asked by your parents to look after the house while they were gone. They and I have been very worried about you."

"What's my father's first name?" Myron asked.

"Irving."

"What's my mother's maiden name?"

"I don't know; she hasn't been known to I for that long. Look, Myron—"

"Which phone are you on?"

"Er. The one in the kitchen."

"Okay. What color is the refrigerator?"

"Myron, there's no time for questions. I can come get you."

"Look at the refrigerator, Mrs. Wangenstein. Tell me what color it is."

"White."

"Wrong answer."

"Myron, I'm colorbli—" But he had already hung up.

He stood at the phone and tried to think. Mrs. Wangenstein had not been in his home, which meant that someone had rerouted his parents' phone number to Mrs. Wangenstein's house, or to her cell. Who would have the resources to switch phone numbers around like that? Was it safe to go back to Westfield? Myron picked up the phone again and called 911. Before he could say a word, however, he felt himself being picked up by the scruff of his neck, which proved to be much more painful than he would have guessed. Mr. Rodriguez was dragging him outside toward the car.

"Help me!" Myron called.

"He's a truant," Mr. Rodriguez reassured the unmoving and uninterested man on the milk crate, "from Estonia." He opened the driver's side door and threw Myron across the stick shift into the passenger seat. The car was already running, and Mr. Rodriguez was driving away before Myron had recovered his wits enough to try the door handle. It was, of course, locked.

"How did you find me? Were you monitoring the phones, too?"

"You ugly freak, of course I was going to find you. There's nowhere else a body can walk to. Now you better tell me who you called."

"No one, you got me right after I dialed."

"Maybe that's true," said Mr. Rodriguez, "but I've got to figure out what to do with you. You know so much about the school operations. I've just got to figure it out."

A few fat, lethargic raindrops struck the windshield. By the time Myron and Mr. Rodriguez had reached the house, it was pouring.

3.

The other kids were scrambling to drag their defenestrated bedrolls into the house before they got too soaked. Myron was sitting in an overstuffed chair, trying desperately to will himself into the form of a wolf. Or a tiger. Or an alligator. Mr. Rodriguez had turned bright flaming red.

"I take you in, I feed and clothe you, and this is the thanks you give me," he roared. "You betray me, you run away, you try to betray our family secrets! I didn't want to hurt you, I wasn't going to do anything to you." Outside, dimly refracted through the pounding rain, lightning momentarily illuminated the sky. "But you forcing my hand, boy!" Then, so loud both of them jumped, the thunder struck.

"I wasn't going to say anything about you, I just wanted to call my parents."

"I'm your parents now, dumb-ass! You don't know how hard this is! I don't know what to do with these kids in December when they have to go home, and then they tell all their friends I don't have no school. I can't let them go, but I can't keep them here another year. And then you have to show up, and you can actually talk normal . . ."

It suddenly occurred to Myron that Mr. Rodriguez was under the impression that the school year started in January, and he began to laugh.

"You won't think it's so funny when you're at the bottom of the river," Mr. Rodriguez was shrieking. He jumped up and began to tremble all over. Myron was scared; he could feel every hair on the back of his neck, where Mr. Rodriguez had picked him up, begin to tingle. Suddenly he remembered feeling this way before. And at that moment a bison came bursting through the wall. Its great head smashed into Mr. Rodriguez and sent him flying to one side. The bison skidded into a bookshelf, and a set of hardcover Time-Life books came tumbling down onto its back. When it turned around, Myron had already darted out the hole in the wall and was running through the rain.

The wind and the driving rain made it hard to see, but Myron was fairly certain that a bison had managed to burst back out of the house and was in pursuit. He could feel it in his hackles. A bison was probably faster than a boy, he figured, so he deliberately headed for the copse of trees he'd passed a couple of hours before. He could hear the bison snorting and the thundering of its hooves close behind him, and he practically dived into the thick tangle of birch branches. Scrambling through the copse, he lit out at an oblique angle to the direction he'd entered, and was soon dodging between the rusted-orange chassis and engine blocks. It was hard to see in the rain, and a black tire, camouflaged against the ground, caught Myron's foot. He went head over heels and was fortunate to land on nothing harder than the deep mud. He was breathing hard, and, in the precious seconds he spent prying himself out of the ground, he could sense his lead evaporating. Indeed, no sooner had he begun to run than he could hear the metallic clanging of a bison ricocheting off the upside-down body of half a minibus. Myron's mud-sodden shoes were making their own noise, a grotesque sucking sound with every step.

"A cheetah, a cheetah," Myron tried, but in vain. He remained a biped, and the bison was gaining.

But there ahead were the railroad tracks, and between him and them the broad ditch. Myron pitched down into it, through the filthy morass at the bottom, and began to mount the far side. Surely a bison would not be able to follow. Maybe Benson could turn into a man and climb around in ditches that way, but, frankly, Myron figured it was better to be pursued by a man than by a solid ton with horns. All these hopes flashed through Myron's mind in the moment he scrambled up the side, but then, with a palpable burst of air pressure, a train came whistling by, less than a foot away. It was a freight train, and boxcar after boxcar sped past, with no end in sight. Myron was cut off.

"All right, it was a nice race, but you're trapped now."

Myron turned at the sound of the voice. There, separated from him only by six feet of ditch, stood, naked, the man who had terrified him in Westfield.

"What do you want?" Myron asked. The din of the rain and the hammering rails meant that he had to shout to be heard.

"The boss is curious about you. So you're coming with me to meet him."

"Is he going to hurt me?" Myron asked. The train was still going, still rumbling past.

"What do I care?"

Myron was desperate to keep Benson talking. Once the train was gone, maybe he could start running again. "How did you find me? What did you do with my parents?"

"You don't have a choice in this, you know," Benson said. And taking a step or two back, and then forward, he launched himself across the ditch, landing close to the speeding train. In the mud he slipped for a moment, and Myron caught his breath, but Benson righted himself. He was now standing right in front of Myron.

"Is it true," Myron asked, "tell me first, is it true that we're immortal lycanthropes?"

"I don't know, or care, what they told you, but I can kill you, you know. I can gore you."

"But you'd have to gore me, right? You can only kill me in animal form."

Benson put his hand out. "Make this easy. Just give me your hand, and we'll go back to the car." Benson's face, and his hand, lit up for a moment as a bolt forked across the sky.

Myron at that moment launched himself sideways, directly at the train. He bounced off the side with a horrible squelch, landed back on his soggy sneakers, tottered a moment, and fell directly back against the train. This time he happened to fall between cars, and with a series of cracks and a great outpouring of blood the front of a box-car slammed into him. He fell down, as loose as a rag doll, gushing blood, but he stayed where he was, stuck on the coupling, as the train dragged him away. Benson stood wet and dumbfounded. Myron's limp body was out of sight by the time the thunder sounded.

III

John Dillinger's Legacy

"He'd make a good boy for our business," said Smith,
   musingly.

Martin shook his head.

"It wouldn't do," he said.

"Why not?"

"He wants to be honest," said Martin, contemptuously.
   "We couldn't trust him."

Horatio Alger, *Rufus and Rose*

I.

Shoreditch, Pennsylvania, was founded as a mining town, and tried, when the coal ran out, to reinvent itself as a manufacturing town. The broken windows of factories and the innumerable corrugated tin shacks, many collapsed into lean-tos or stacks of tin sheets, offered the evidence of this plan's failure, and of a chronology of decay. A Heinrich Schliemann of the future would find the layers of this Troy, the layers of splendor and squalor, coexisting and overlapping—with squalor, as it always does, gradually taking over. And there in Shoreditch central stood the Grand Lafayette, four glorious stories of memories of better times, or at least better times for some. The doorman still dressed like an Austro-Hungarian admiral, and the remaining crystal prisms in the grand chandelier still twinkled in the high cracked ceilings of the lobby. The Grand Lafayette had in its day been a swank hotel, then a swank convention center, then a swank apartment building, and if it had seen better days, so have we all, and it was still the swankest place in Shoreditch.

In the penthouse of the Grand Lafayette sat a rather dusty apartment crammed to the gills with curios and knickknacks. An art deco version of an Egyptian woman, five feet tall, balanced a lamp on her head, all hand-cast in bronze. A stuffed impala's head, one glass eye long since having fallen out, overlooked a life-size pair of ceramic dalmatians and a score of tiny angel statues, Manchurian vase-ware, glass kittens, monogrammed letter openers in gold leaf (fanned out into an "attractive display"), Hopi kachina dolls, and one wind-up singing bird. The carpets were exquisite, Persian, and threadbare. On the walls hung faded satin-cut silhouettes in tarnished frames and pre-Raphaelite maidens in gilded frames; over the windows hung thick flowered curtains. A large sepia globe that still maintained the memory of the Polish corridor had proved to be hinged, and it hung open, revealing inside a collection of whisky bottles, half full; or perhaps, in Shoreditch, half empty. Several other bottles had clearly been emptied recently, and were scattered around a leather easy chair. In the leather chair sat, passed out, a woman in late middle age, barefoot, a velvet dressing gown tied around her and a cigarette, smoldering between her fingers. Two other partially smoked and still glowing cigarettes had been put out in an open nearby jewelry box, the kind that played a tune when the lid was up. It was still tinkling away when

Myron Horowitz eased through the penthouse door. He sat unseen on the ottoman and waited in silence. He'd gotten good at waiting. The woman was black, her wrinkled skin very dark, and the dressing gown, like the chair, was red.

After a few minutes, the jewelry box stopped, in the middle of a measure. The woman started, leaned over, ground her cigarette in the box, and then held it up to wind it. Partway through, she stopped. Slowly, she began to lift her head.

"What song is that?" Myron asked.

The woman shoved hard with her feet, and the chair tipped over backwards. Springing up on the far side of the clattering chair was no woman but an enormous gorilla, its lips pulled back to display yellow fangs. The sight might have been terrifying, except the gorilla was ludicrously wearing a dressing gown, now ill-fitted to simian proportions.

"Arthur and Alice sent me," Myron said.

The gorilla lifted the fallen chair upright. Suddenly a woman was wearing the dressing gown again. She tugged it back into place. "You must be Myron Lipschitz."

"Myron Horowitz."

"Well, that's a little better. How did you get in here?"

"The doorman didn't say anything. No one thinks a kid like me is up to trouble, as long as I keep my back to him. And the door to this apartment was unlocked."

The woman darted to the door, opened it, bent down stiffly to grab some shoes, drew them into the room, and locked the door.

"What," Myron asked, "do they shine your shoes if you leave them outside?"

"No, but they used to, forty years ago. I guess I just put them out on instinct and forgot to lock up behind me." The woman groped around on the floor for a glass and began to fix a drink from the bottles in the globe. "Hair of the dog. You want some?"

"I'm just a kid."

"Suit yourself." She stirred the concoction with a letter opener.

"Um. Are you Gloria?"

"Maybe. How'd you find me?"

"I had a talk, a while ago, with Arthur and Alice, and I've gone over what they said a million times in my head since then. And one thing I remember them mentioning was a Gloria in Shoreditch."

"And then what, you just wandered around town until you got that prickling sensation in your nose?"

"I get it on the back of my neck. But yeah. It took me three days."

Gloria gave him the once-over. "You don't look like you've been sleeping on the street."

"I stole these clothes from a Laundromat this morning. And it's too cold to sleep on the street, I've mainly been in garages."

"Laundromat, huh? You're okay. Anyone resourceful at expropriation is okay in my book. So what else did Arthur tell you about me?"

"Nothing much. All I know about you is that you're a friend of theirs."

"I'm a friend of Arthur's, not Alice's. Remember that, you can't trust her."

"I can trust Arthur, though, then?"

"Well, no, not really." She began to laugh, at first a little and then increasingly hysterically, until she choked on her drink. When she was done, she said, "You do look like you've been hit by a truck."

"It was a train, actually. Look, I have a lot of questions for you."

Gloria closed her eyes and tilted her head back. "Ask 'em. I've got all night."

"You can't have all night, it's almost noon."

Gloria jumped up and ran over to the window. She shuffled when she walked, like an old woman, but Myron remembered the few moments when she was a gorilla, and how differently, how fluidly she had moved. She was now pulling open the curtains, and when the noonday sun struck her in the face, she closed her eyes and gasped. Her pupils, when she turned back around, were contracted into pinpoints.

She said, "We've got to get out of here."

"Okay, let's go."

"I can't go out the front, they know me."

"We could just stay here," Myron suggested.

"No, the owners might be back at any minute."

"You . . . don't live here?"

"Of course not, look at this place! It's bourgeois tacky!"

"That's a nice painting," Myron said, pointing over at the corner.

Gloria was gathering up some things and throwing them into a sack. "That's not a painting, that's a print."

"No, it's not. Prints have the name of the museum on the bottom."

"Faith, Myron! What are you? Are you a bat or something?"

"I don't know yet."

"Okay, go through the lobby. I'll meet you out on the street, around the corner. Do you have any money on you?"

"No."

"Okay, I'll meet you anyway." She turned back to the window. "I hate doing this in daylight," she said.

And then a gorilla was shucking off the dressing gown. With the sack over her shoulder, she jumped out the window.

2.

Gloria was dressed when Myron saw her again, and she kept looking behind her. "I hate doing that," she said.

"In daylight. I know," said Myron.

Gloria turned back to the boy. "You've got a mouth on you."

Myron was suddenly embarrassed. "I guess I do. I didn't used to."

"Okay, let's get some money and then go to a diner and get some coffee."

"Get some money how?"

And then for twenty minutes Myron stood on the curb while Gloria accosted passersby and asked, in his name, for spare change. "A deaf mute, permanently maimed by an exploding stove! Please have a heart! The shoddy Japanese manufacturers refused to pay him a cent! The explosion claimed the lives of his parents, and the poor little crippled orphan will never see them again!" Soon Myron legitimately began to cry, and that didn't hurt the game at all. After twenty minutes, Gloria dragged Myron across town to a diner.

"Mass! Look at this haul! Your face is your fortune, Myron." She ordered two bacon and egg sandwiches and two coffees. "All right, tell me your story. How'd you get here?"

"It is a shameful fact about humanity," Myron did not say. This is not the "Repunnotunkur" here. Instead he began to talk about Westfield, and Henry Clay High School.

"No, no, Arthur already told me all about that," Gloria said, unaware that I had made up most of the stuff I told her, to cover up my own ignorance, and may have even gotten Myron's last name wrong. "What happened—what happened after you fell out of the truck?"

"I woke up in a ditch, and this guy found me. He ran a kind of fraudulent school, where international students would come, and then he'd steal all their money while they just kind of foraged for themselves."

"Sure, the Featherstone Academy."

"You know it?"

"Waiter! More coffee! I make it a habit to know people, especially people who are stupid and have money."

"Okay. I was all banged up, but I rested at the academy for a while. But then this guy Benson—you know Benson?"

"Of *course* I know Benson."

"Well, he found me there and chased me over to the railroad tracks. Then I jumped on a train. Or kind of in front of a train. And that hurt worse than anything, but it got me away. And I rested up again and found you."

"First things first." Gloria was lighting a cigarette and trying to inhale while she talked. "Benson didn't find you. Benson couldn't find his shaggy hump with a map and a two-hour head start. Mignon Emanuel found you, and she sent Benson to do her dirty work, a mistake you can bet she won't make again."

"Benson works for Mignon Emanuel?"

"No, they both work for Mr. Bigshot. But Benson would listen to Mignon Emanuel. He's just smart enough to know what he's not smart enough to do on his own; which is, frankly, smarter than usual."

"Right, Mr. Bigshot. I guess I knew that."

"Second things second. You left out how you recovered the second time, after the train. I presume you did not go back to Andre Rodriguez?"

Myron paused a moment. He sampled the coffee, which was still too hot. Some things, he was learning, are hard to talk about. Finally he said, "I read this book once, about these three hunters in the American frontier, and one of them got mauled by a bear. It was a terrible mauling, and he was in real bad shape, and then his wounds get infected, and he gets the fever. His friends can't get him to move, and there's nothing they can do for him anyway, so they camp out and wait for him either to get better or die. But the thing is, is it's Indian country, and every day they wait puts them all into more and more incredible danger. Finally, it looks like the guy—his name was Hugh Glass—"

"(This is a true story, now?)"

"(Yeah, this was a nonfiction book.) It looks like Hugh Glass is going to die any moment, and he's in a coma and everything. So his two friends can't wait any longer—they decide to just leave him, assuming he'll be dead in the morning. And they take all his gear, and his gun and everything, and they book. But the next morning, Glass's fever breaks. And he realizes that his friends have gone, that they've left him alone with no gun and no food, and he *vows revenge!*" Myron was getting into the story. "Glass crawls around till he finds a spring, and he lies in the underbrush, eating all the berries he can reach, and gulping at the spring, until he's strong enough to sit up; and then he can reach more berries! And bit by bit his strength returns. He's still ripped to shreds, and his face is mostly off, but his strength returns until he can stagger around, and he happens to come across where some wolves had killed a deer or something, and he comes running out screaming at them, and one look at this guy, and the wolves turn tail and run, so he gets some meat. And he looks so terrifying, like a zombie, that the Indians don't want to kill him, and he goes walking through the frontier, looking to find the two guys who abandoned him."

"Did he find them?"

"Yeah, but it took forever, and he forgave them in the end. You know how that goes."

"Myron, why are you telling me this story?"

"Because after a few miles I fell off the train. And after a while I could think and see again, and I dragged myself to a muddy ditch. And then I dragged myself away from the tracks, in case Benson was looking for me, along the tracks. And I found a barberry bush, and I ate the berries until I could sit up."

"Too bad they sent Benson, and not a bloodhound, huh?"

"Does a bloodhound work for Mr. Bigshot?"

"No, I was just talking. There is no bloodhound."

"Oh. Well, it was raining anyway, for a long time. I was just afraid Benson would come by and sense me. How come there's no bloodhound?"

"Faith, I don't know, a bloodhound's just a kind of dog. There's just one of us per species."

"Why is that?"

"That's just the way it is. You might as well ask why people walk on their feet, and not their hands."

"If people walked on their hands, wouldn't they just call hands *feet?*"

"I mean," Gloria said, lighting a cigarette off the last one, "that this all happened so long ago that no one knows, and if they ever did know, they don't remember."

"How old are you?"

"Same age as you, probably. Ten thousand years or so."

"You don't know how old you are?"

"Myron, darling, it's easy to lose count with numbers that big. Also, when I was born I doubt if there were any languages on Earth that could count as high as ten thousand. And who knows for how long I just lived as a gorilla, living among gorillas, not even knowing humans were anything except another thing to run away from, or rip apart?"

"Am I that old, too?"

"Either that or you're the first one of us to be born since anyone knew to keep track. Which actually isn't that long ago, so it might not be ridiculous."

"It isn't that long?"

"Until two or three thousand years ago, I never left the jungle. Eventually I went exploring, but I was still in Africa, in the lakes region and then the Kalahari. If anything was happening anywhere else in the world, I sure didn't know about it. The idea that there were a finite number of us, that there were one per species, nobody figured that out until the eighteenth or nineteenth century, probably."

"Well, why are we? I mean, why are we this way?"

"Why are anyone the way they are, Myron? When I first met humans, I was worshiped as a god. I don't even remember this part so well. They taught me to speak, but I hated my human form, it was so weak and clumsy. I was already old. My human skin was always old."

"Why do you live among humans now, then?"

Gloria shrugged. "I like indoor plumbing. I like coffee and cigarettes. I like movies. There are perks."

"I guess we can't die?"

"Oh, you can die all right. But you can only get killed by another one of us, and only if he's in animal form. I could turn right now and tear you to bits, and that would be the end of you. Plenty of us have died—we'll probably never know how many. Any number of immortal rodents or shrews might have been killed by immortal cats before either even knew they could change. And in the last few hundred years, when we started being able really to travel—there've been a lot of deaths in the last few hundred years. Most of the seals got killed by the polar bear, and the polar bear got killed by a rhinoceros, the kind with one horn. And Mr. Bigshot killed her."

"But that stuff, the claws and the bite, is that the only way to die?"

"I wouldn't go jumping in any volcanoes to test this, but you do tend to heal fast from any other kind of wound. Have you ever been hurt badly, I mean before the train thing?"

"I once almost choked to death on a piece of ice."

"And what happened?"

"Well, it was ice. It melted in my throat, and I was fine."

"That's a bad example, then."

"And I've been beaten up a lot . . ."

"The point is," said Gloria, "you're not in much danger from conventional methods of dying."

"What about what happened to me before all that? I mean, my accident."

"Well, that was Mr. Bigshot. That was a lion."

"Benson said I fought a lion and its mane, but I couldn't figure out what he meant."

"No, no, Myron, you fought a lion in Maine."

"Oh. That's where they found me, in Maine."

"Yeah, five years ago Mr. Bigshot, apparently, sensed someone new, an animal he'd never sensed before, but in human form. That was you, whatever you were doing there. He mauled you, but you fell in a river, and, well, Mr. Bigshot hates water. So you floated away toward the sea."

"I thought lions didn't hate water, that's just a myth."

"Mr. Bigshot hates water. I don't know anything about other lions."

"So I floated away, but I didn't die."

"No, but you didn't heal up, either, because your wounds are from lion's claws. Look." Gloria pointed a knobby, swollen finger at Myron's face and traced, one by one, the parallel scars. "It was all the gossip at the time, how Mr. Bigshot found someone new, and killed him."

"I fought a lion and lost."

"Everybody who fights the lion loses. Seventy-five years ago he killed the tiger, which no one thought he'd be able to do. But he did it."

"What was the tiger's name?"

"You know that he didn't really have a name. He was a tiger."

"Oh, I thought because you have a name—"

"Gloria's not my name. They just call me Gloria because it's convenient. Do you think they called me Gloria in Bantu a thousand years ago? How long do you think Benson has been called Benson? The tiger was going by the name Bima, but he might as well have been Shere Khan. Bima wasn't his name, and Arthur isn't his name, and Myron isn't yours. They're just a tiger, or a binturong, or whatever you are."

"Yeah, what am I?"

"I guess we could go through every animal I've known who isn't you, and eliminate them. But that might not help, since I couldn't name every mammal, and there might have been some that died before we knew about them, and there might be some we just don't know because they're isolated, or in hiding, or never show up for reasons of their own. And it's not always easy to tell how many there are supposed to be. I mean, there are supposedly three species of zebra, I saw on the TV, but I've only known one immortal zebra. Are the other two dead, or in hiding, or did they never exist, and you only get one zebra? I don't know."

"So I could be anything."

"Well, you couldn't be a prairie dog, and you couldn't be a jaguar, and you couldn't be a hippopotamus, because I know all of those. It's hard to tell your ethnicity, without a face, but your skin's too light to be from some places, if you wanted to cross off those possibilities. So there are lots of things you couldn't be, but there are still lots of things you could be."

"Okay, just two more questions. Why did Mr. Bigshot want to kill me?"

"Maybe you were talking dirt about his mother. But probably he just wanted to know what you were. When we die we turn back into our true form. Curiosity, you know."

"Because cats are curious?"

Gloria was obviously beginning to get bored, looking around the room. "Mr. Bigshot is curious. I don't know about other cats. He's probably still interested, plus he's mad about you thwarting him once, or three times now. And he must've read about you ripping all your clothes off, at your school. Ripped clothes are a sure sign one of us is around."

"Arthur changed, but he didn't rip his clothes."

"Binturongs are small. I split a seam on the robe I was wearing, and that was a loose robe too big for me. Trust me, mention ripped clothes and all of us know what's up."

"How does Mr. Bigshot have people work for him? Is it because he's the king of the beasts?"

"Don't be ridiculous, I don't have a king. I was a queen, once upon a time, but I don't have a king. Mr. Bigshot has minions because he can beat everyone else up, now that the tiger's gone. Or else no one wants to try their luck on him. So when he says he's in charge, he's in charge until someone comes around who'll say no." Gloria stood up. "I'm paying the check, you leave the tip."

"I don't have any money."

Gloria sighed and dropped a dollar on the table. "Well, do you have any other questions?"

"I don't know, um. Why is this place called Shoreditch? We're nowhere near the shore."

"It's named after some part of London. Okay, it was great to meet you, Myron. I hope I was able to fill in some things for you. Best of luck."

"Wait, you can't leave yet."

"Don't worry, I'm just going to pay the check." But she didn't pay the check; she just left.

3.

The waiter accosted Myron when he tried to go, but he couldn't bring himself to actually touch the boy, so Myron walked out unhindered. He had a lot to think over, but he was also in a state of panic. His whole plan, since he dragged himself away from the train tracks, had been to go to Shoreditch and ask Gloria what to do next. And now as it turned out, it wasn't that she didn't know what to do; she just didn't seem to care.

Myron ran down the street, looking all around. Not long after he'd been adopted, when Myron was still so very confused and even spoke with a strange accent that some people said sounded Canadian, the Horowitzes had taken him to an amusement park. Already dizzy from the teacups, Myron had wandered away from his new parents in the crowd, and the half-hour before he, or rather a security guard, found them again was filled not so much with terror—terror is so common an emotion among children that a terrifying day is hardly remarkable—as with despair. This, despair, Myron was becoming reacquainted with as he tore through the streets of Shoreditch. Except he was hardly aware, yet, that it was despair he was becoming reacquainted with. He was too terrified.

With just such a complicated mixture of emotions blinding him, Myron knocked over two perverts and a policeman (who was too fat to follow him) and managed to avoid, narrowly, being squashed by a plumber's van. "Gloria!" he shouted, again and again, and then he stopped, when he remembered that this was not even her name. She had no name, and neither did he.

Finally, out of breath, and growing leery of the many glares that a deformed, careless, running boy will garner, he slowed down to a walk. He had found Gloria once before, he could find her again the same way, if he wanted to. But it was clear, he'd decided, that Gloria was unreliable, and he was probably better off contriving a new plan, without her.

So of course, no sooner had he decided this than he rounded a corner and, his hackles suddenly tingling, he saw across the street Gloria, with her sack, bumping into a well-dressed man. A pair of glasses fell off her head and hit the sidewalk with a crunch.

That's odd, Myron doubtless thought. *I didn't know she wore glasses.*

"Sir! You've broken my spectacles!" Gloria, meanwhile, was shouting.

"Er, I'm sorry? But you bumped into me."

"Impossible! I was standing still, and you walked right into me." Gloria really chewed the scenery. She needed these glasses for her job as a bus driver for the orphanage. She could not afford another pair, and without the money bus driving brought in she would not be able to afford her dialysis. Also, the orphans would not be able to get to the clinic to be treated for their eczema.

"This is all very sad, but I did not bump into you. And how bad could their eczema be, anyway?"

At that moment Gloria turned around. She pointed right at Myron. "Johnny!" she called. "This man broke my glasses, and I can't get you to the clinic!"

"Good Lord!" cried the man.

And, after the man had departed, Gloria sauntered over to Myron, counting the roll of bills. "Bourgeois idiot, he's obviously not from around here," she was muttering.

"Why did you leave?" Myron asked.

Gloria shrugged. "I figured I'd already told you everything you needed to know."

"You stuck me with—"

"Okay, so I didn't want to pay the check. I figured they wouldn't make you, I figured the waiter'd be too busy looking at you to recognize me if I came back in. Once the idea got in my head, it seemed too good an opportunity to pass up."

"What about the help you're supposed to give me? Why did Arthur want to bring me to you if this is all you can do for me?"

She secreted the bills somewhere under her neckline. "Mass, Myron, you don't think Arthur was really bringing you to me?"

"He said he was heading for Gloria in Shoreditch. How else would I have found you?"

"He didn't want to bring you to me, he just wanted his doomsday device back."

"Doomsday device?" Myron shook his head. "This just gets stupider and stupider. Did you give him the doomsday device?"

"Of course not," Gloria said. "I haven't seem him in seven or eight years. And when I saw him last, that's when he gave me the device."

"You're just telling me lies, aren't you? How did he tell you all about me, like you've been claiming he did, if he didn't come right here after he lost me?"

"Myron, you have to start thinking things through better. You could be in real danger if you act stupid like this. He phoned me, of course. He called me from the road. What year do you think this is?"

"Oh," Myron said.

"Anyway, he'd know better than to bring that doxy around me."

"Are you . . . Are you *jealous* of them?"

"Myron, come here." Gloria pulled him over to a side street and began walking him along, at a fairly rapid clip considering the way she hobbled. She leaned in to whisper in his ear. "You have to understand this. There's nothing to be jealous about. Arthur and Alice aren't dating. Binturongs and lesser pandas don't date. That would be bestiality—or double bestiality—or whatever it would be, animals don't get turned on across species."

"Oh."

"Maybe that's what you should do, to figure out what kind you are. Walk around the zoo until you feel something stirring." She laughed and actually elbowed Myron in the ribs as they were walking, making him stagger several steps. "I told you to get smarter, Myron. You're going to need it." She suddenly stopped and, painfully bending over, began rummaging around in her sack, which she was still toting.

"Gloria, I don't know what to do. A lion wants to kill me, and I can't find my parents, and I've never been on a trip alone before."

"Chin up, Myron. If you ever had parents, they died ten thousand years ago. Now, I can't tell you what to do, because if I knew I wouldn't be a drunk and a gambler and a thief."

"You're a thief?"

"Not really—really I'm an expropriator, and a propagandist. A propagandist by the deed."

"What does that mean?"

"It means where did you get those clothes?" She drew from the sack a cylinder about fifteen inches long and six inches in diameter, wrapped in black duct tape. "I can't tell you what to do, but here's something, maybe it'll keep you busy. You can take this doomsday device and deliver it to Arthur."

Myron took the cylinder gingerly. "What's in here?"

They were walking again, Gloria pulling Myron along by the sleeve. "John Dillinger's wang," she said.

"What!"

"No, I mean, faith, I don't know. I never open anything I've heard called a doomsday device."

"I don't know where Arthur is."

"Well, he's looking for you, too, so that should double your chances. And what you can do is ask the Nine Unknown Men, they always know this kind of thing."

"I don't know who they are, either."

"You're not supposed to, naturally; they're unknown. They're in New York City, at the corner of Fifth Street and Sixth Avenue. You should be writing this down."

"I don't have a pencil. Literally the only things I own in this world are these stolen clothes and a doomsday device."

"You do have a mouth on you. Let's hope you have a brain, too."

"Corner of Fifth Street and Sixth Avenue."

"Good. Now the Nine Unknown Men will ask you a riddle, and if you get it right they'll help you, but if you get it wrong—well, you don't want to get it wrong. Are you good at riddles?"

"Yes."

"Good. Now listen closely, because this is the most important thing I'm going to tell you. Do you remember that print in the apartment you found me in? The one you said was a painting?"

"Sure."

"There are certain classes of people who will buy original art but can't bring themselves to own a reproduction. It's 'vulgar,' or 'common,' to own a reproduction of the *Mona Lisa,* even though of course no one could possibly afford the original *Mona Lisa.* So what do you think they do, Myron?"

"A reproduction?"

"I mean a poster of the *Mona Lisa,* not the original."

"Yes, I know what a reproduction is," Myron sniffed. "I just don't understand why you're telling me this."

"What they do is they buy a poster of the *Mona Lisa,* but one that has at the bottom a notation that says what exhibit it's from. This way they can pretend that it's not a poster of the *Mona Lisa,* which is too vulgar for words, but a promotional item, like a movie poster or a concert poster. A souvenir of their trip to the Louvre. It's a kind of trick. The people who adopted you, Myron—"

"My parents."

"The people who adopted you. They're upper middle class, aren't they?"

"I don't know. My father's a doctor."

"All the art in their house, I'm betting, was either an actual painting or a poster that said 'Philadelphia Museum of Art,' with the date, on the bottom."

"Maybe."

"You've got to understand, not everyone is like that. Not everyone refuses to hang posters up. Some people are petit bourgeois and not haut bourgeois. Not everyone is going to be from the same world you know. *You're* not from the same world you know. Remember that. Ah. Up you go now."

Myron found that Gloria was muscling him onto a bus. She slipped him a roll of twenties bound with a rubber band.

"This goes to New York," she said. "I'll take care of your ticket. The Nine Unknown Men, don't forget them, either."

"Wait, why am I giving Arthur this doomsday device? What should I do about the lion?"

"You've got plenty of options. Maybe you can use the doomsday device to get revenge, like Hugh Jass."

"Hugh Glass."

Gloria nodded appreciatively. "Well, that's a little better."

No one sat next to Myron. One person tried, but he threw up and had to change seats. After an hour on the bus, Myron thought to look closer at the roll of twenties. He found that only the top bill was a twenty; the other eight were singles. When he got to New York he learned that Gloria had not paid for the ticket; she had somehow persuaded the driver that some guardian of Myron's would pay double on arrival. While the driver called the station police, Myron ran away into the cold and shadowy night.

IV

Men, Known and Unknown

New men and new methods might do for other people:
let those who would, worship the rising star; he at least
would be faithful to the sun which had set.

Thomas Hughes, *Tom Brown's School Days*

I.

I have written under a great host of pseudonyms in my day.
Plentygood van Dutchhook, "Fortitude," A. Frederick Smith,
G. A. Henty, Lawrence Christopher Niffen, Frank Richards,
Vivian Bloodmark, and, briefly, Wen Piao, are just a few of
my more popular noms de plume; but I hit my greatest cir-
culation ghostwriting for the Stratameyer syndicate. There I,
or rather we, for I was one of a stable of anonymous ghost-
writers, churned out a great many stories of young men and
women solving mysteries, sometimes inventing things, and
always, always triumphing over mild to severe adversity. For
Stratameyer alone I must have written a dozen scenes of
urchins forced to spend the night on the forbidding pave-
ments of New York. But frankly, I was whitewashing the
experience.

Myron, who may have read a dozen such scenes, had

no way of knowing that. He had of late spent many nights sleeping outside, and had thought he had become inured to its hardships. But that night in New York, huddled amid the steam oozing through a grating, was the longest, the coldest, and the most terrible night of his life. Gripping tightly the garbage bag he'd stashed the doomsday device in, he waited for doomsday. "I cannot die, I cannot die," he muttered to himself, as he rocked back and forth. And then people came out of the dark and tried to prove him wrong.

But the streetlight turned around and shone itself dead on Myron's face. And so the people, their attempts were desultory.

There is an old Islamic folktale about a man who, having burned in hell for what feels like a thousand years, is given a chance to speak to the living. "How many thousand years have I been dead?" he asks them; and they answer, "A day, and part of a day." That was Myron's night, it was a day and part of a day.

The first thing he did when he woke up was eat three hot dogs, courtesy of Gloria's money and a nearby street vendor, and the second thing was ask a dozen people for increasingly circuitous directions to the public library. There he looked up and read through several books of riddles. He wanted to take them out, but he didn't think his tattered Pennsylvania library card would work. He wanted to stop and maybe read an adventure novel, but he knew he didn't have time. He had work to do. He tried looking up, on the computer catalog, the Nine Unknown Men. Nothing came up, but Myron wasn't sure he was doing it right—was *nine* spelled out or should it be a numeral? Finally he gave up and headed over to the dusty, disrepaired card catalog, kept in ancient wooden drawers in a strange corner of the third floor. He opened up the *N* drawer and flipped through. Sure enough, *Nine Unknown Men* had its own card, and when he touched it, he heard a tinkling sound. A tiny bell had been threaded through a hole punched in the card, and it sounded when the card moved.

Suddenly an old man in a plaid suit and a porkpie hat appeared behind Myron. "You probably don't want to mess around with those reprobates," he said.

Myron stared at him. His hackles were still. The man was not one of them, not a lycanthrope.

"Here's a card," the man said, flipping one out from inside his plaid sleeve. The card read A. WEISHAUPT & CO., ILLUMINATIONS. "These guys are pretty swell. Would you like a bowl of soup?"

Myron said he would not.

"So anyway, if you don't mind my asking, why were you interested in the Nine Unknown Men?"

"I wasn't," Myron lied. "I was just flipping around. I'm really looking for information on John Dillinger."

"Ah," said the man, nodding his head. His tie was very wide, and a hula girl was painted on it. Myron looked closely to make certain, as he didn't want to make a mistake after

Gloria's lecture, but he could see the streaks of paint. The tie had been hand painted. "Dillinger," the man continued, adjusting his horn-rimmed glasses, "is quite the berries."

"Quite the berries?"

"I merely mean that he is a fascinating subject. Some say he killed JFK, but I think we can agree that's an exaggeration, eh?" He chuckled, and looked expectantly at Myron. He looked him right in the face, which most people, on the first day, cannot do.

"I have to go now," Myron said. And he went to the corner of Fifth Street and Sixth Avenue. The walk took him over an hour, and he got lost for part of it, when a man in a battered fedora and a seersucker suit talked him into walking six blocks and one mysterious flight of stairs in the wrong direction, but at last he found himself at his destination. On one of the four corners was a deli; on two others, pornography stores. The fourth corner had a plain brick building with a small bronze plaque that read 9UM. There was no bell, so Myron pulled the marbled glass door open. The small lobby contained a dying, beribboned potted plant; a slouched-over janitor, his cap pulled low, polishing the floor with a huge buzzing machine; and a high white marbled desk, behind which sat a smartly dressed man. The man had a little mustache and a headphone over one ear. There was very little room for Myron in the lobby.

Myron figured he might as well just cut right to the chase. "I'm here to see the Nine Unknown Men," he said.

"If they are unknown, this may prove difficult," the man behind the desk said. He had an Indian accent.

"It's cool, Gloria sent me," Myron said, loudly to be heard over the floor polisher.

He paused a moment, and seemed to be listening on his earpiece. "You have told one lie today, Myron Horowitz," the man said inexplicably. "Tell another and you must face the web of silver."

"No, no." Myron could barely see over the lip of the white desk. "I'm one of those . . . I don't even know what to call them." He tried to lean forward for a conspiratorial whisper, but he was too short. "I'm an immortal lycanthrope."

"That will get you through the door," the man said, and he moved his hands around behind the desk, where Myron couldn't see. Perhaps he pressed a button, because a panel in the wall, behind the dying plant, slid open, and he tilted his head toward it.

Myron had to clamber over the plant to enter. He found himself, as the door slid shut behind him, in a small pitch-black room. Suddenly his ears were popping, and he realized he was in an elevator, descending rapidly. He was blinded momentarily when the door opened again. Here was a larger, brighter lobby. People were walking quickly back and forth, carrying clipboards and pocket calculators. Most of them looked Indian. A woman, wrapped in a brightly colored dress, gestured for Myron to follow her. She was wearing a security badge, with her photo and the name Sukumarika on it. The two walked down a long white corridor that reminded Myron of the hospital.

"Listen carefully," said the woman, Sukumarika, "because what you are about to hear is non-negotiable, and I will not repeat it. The Nine Unknown Men have been around since before your great-grandmother's great-grandmother was born, and don't think just because you got through the door that we'll change for you."

"If I'm immortal, aren't I older than the Nine Unknown Men?" Myron asked. The woman stopped dead in her tracks.

"I suppose that's correct," she said after a moment, and began walking again. Her lips were pursed disapprovingly, probably because Myron had said *aren't I* instead of *am I not*.

"Actually, I'm not that old," Myron said. "I'm only thirteen."

"You can't be thirteen," Sukumarika said. "None of your kind has been born in millennia."

"Maybe I was just born, maybe I'm the first of a whole new set. Did you ever think of that?"

"This is impossible. The lycanthropes are a dead branch; a dead branch, like the Illuminati."

Myron said, "I don't know what you mean. I was thinking maybe I was more like the chosen one."

At that moment Sukumarika threw a bag over Myron's head. Myron was small enough, and the bag was large enough, that it went down to his waist. He tried struggling, but several pairs of hands had seized him, and, mostly from fear, he lost consciousness.

2.

Myron finally found himself in front of a giant metal head, about eight feet tall. It was a woman's head, the color of bronze. The eyes glowed, and the mouth was on a hinge, so it moved, laboriously, when she spoke. She was speaking.

"Myron Horowitz, you have already told one lie today," thundered the brazen head.

"What's happening?" asked Myron, who vaguely assumed, incorrectly, that he was hallucinating.

"Tell another," the voice echoed as it spoke, "and you will face the web of silver."

"I didn't lie, Gloria really sent me."

"This is not the incident to which we refer. Earlier today, in a library, you told one lie. Above all else the Nine Unknown Men demand absolute truth."

"What's the web of silver? Are you one of the Nine Unknown Men? Am I wearing ice skates?"

Myron felt a hand on his shoulder. Only then did he realize that Sukumarika was standing behind him. He had been looking down at his feet. He was wearing not his normal clothes but rather what appeared to be white pajamas, belted at the waist. On his feet were strange boots that looked like skates: to the sole was attached a hook of metal shaped like a sideways U. As soon as he realized how precariously he was balanced on them, he began to wobble.

Sukumarika was whispering in his ear, "Don't be disrespectful. The web of silver is a monofilament mesh at the bottom of a deep pit. The monofilament wire is invisible, except when moistened with dew, whereupon it glistens silver in the light. Anyone who disobeys is dropped in the pit, and at the bottom, he passes through the slicing of the web . . ."

"The experience can be quite straining," the head thundered again. Myron turned toward it, but it gave no indication, by smirk or wink, that it was joking.

"O puissant Meridiana," Sukumarika said, addressing the head for the first time. "Lord Hanusa, whose name is Wrath, is far from us, on secret tasks. Give us your council, most revered one, for before you stands one who claims to be an ancient representative of the lycanthropes."

"Actually, I'm not so ancient, I'm only thirteen. My thesis is that I am some kind of chosen one, the first to be born in a thousand thousand years." Myron, unsteady on his skates, was just the right height to look directly into the head's glowing eyes, and they seemed to him to blaze dangerously as he talked.

"Speak of what you want," Sukumarika hissed in Myron's ear.

"I'm looking for Arthur the binturong, and Alice the red panda," Myron said. "Or even just what to do. Someone wants to kill me and I'm so confused."

"First, you must give the test of the riddle!" intoned the brazen head.

"I must what now?" Myron asked.

"It means," Sukumarika hissed again, "you must face the test."

"If I lose, do I get the web?"

"No," said Sukumarika. "Something worse."

"I'm ready," said Myron, mentally preparing himself.

A faint whirring sound issued from the brazen head. "Which is lighter," spoke the head, its bronze lips opening and closing upon the hinge, "a pound of alabaster or a pound of raven feathers?"

Myron puffed himself up. This was easier than he'd feared. "No problem. They're both the same weight: a pound is always a pound."

"Incorrect. Alabaster is white; raven feathers are black. Alabaster is therefore lighter. He has failed the first test. Now he struggles for his life in the Upside-down Chamber. Take him away."

"What? No fair!" Sukumarika was bringing out her bag. "Don't I get to ask you one? You have to answer my riddle, smarty."

From the head came a puff of air that might have been a sigh. "Very well," it boomed. "Ask your question also."

Myron cleared his throat. He began: "Thirty white horses upon a red—"

"Teeth," said the head. "Take him away." And the bag went on him.

Myron kept shouting riddles from inside the bag as unseen hands bore him away. "I don't bite a man unless he bites me—"

"An onion," Sukumarika said.

"The longer I stand, the shorter—"

"A candle."

"Um. What have I got in my pocket?"

"Nineteen dollars and a card from the Illuminati. We went through your pants."

"Oh. What kind of animal am I?"

"Trivia facts are not riddles."

"But I just wanted to know," said Myron.

When he was unbagged he was in yet another white room. From the ceiling hung dozens of metal rings. He was on a small platform in front of a wide, yawning pit.

Maybe the web of silver won't kill me, Myron thought. *Maybe I'm a starfish.* He had forgotten that starfish are not mammals, and that he was not bound for the silver web. Out loud, Myron said, "I don't want to face the silver web"; but of course he was not going to. For this was the Upside-down Chamber. And so he was hoisted up, turned topsy-turvy, and the U-shaped hooks on his feet slid into the ceiling's metal rings. For the first time Myron saw the men who had been carrying him; huge, burly men with angry faces. Sukumarika was right underneath him, and he grabbed her head for balance. She disentangled herself from him and stepped away, but now her hair stuck out at crazy angles.

"Stop that," she said, trying to smooth her 'do.

"Why are you doing this?" Myron said. He was willing himself vainly to turn into an orangutan, so that he could swing away across the rings.

"Every time I tried to explain, you kept interrupting with

questions." Sukumarika handed him a stout stick, about five feet long.

"I won't interrupt now. I'm really scared."

"Our ways are ancient, passed down from the times of the Emperor Asoka. We do not need to explain them to you."

"So I might as well interrupt, then. Who's Hanusa?"

"Look before you, Myron." Sukumarika pointed across the room. Some thirty yards away, across the pit, on another small platform, a young man wearing identical skates was standing. He was probably only seventeen or eighteen, but to a high school freshman he looked like a grownup. He turned his back on Myron, reached up, grabbed two rings, and pulled himself up so he could hook his feet in the rings. When he let go with his hands, he was hanging upside down, facing forward. He reached down and picked up a staff that had been lying there. The U on the skates was shaped with the mouth forward, toward the toe, so he had to slide his skate backwards, out of the ring, and then forward, to the next ring, in order to advance. He was now out from over the platform, above the pit.

"The pit is filled with spikes," said Sukumarika.

"I'm getting a headache, I think I should get down now," Myron said. Just then, the young man started to run forward. Running must have been very difficult, since he was hanging upside down by hooks on his feet over a spiked pit, but he was good at it. Myron was so startled by the sudden advance, he instinctively flinched backwards. Of course, the skates slipped from the rings, and Myron fell down on the platform with a terrific clatter. His stick rolled into the pit. Everything had to stop while the men came from behind various trapdoors and arras and hoisted Myron up again. They gave him a new stick. After a brief discussion, they started to poke Myron with goads. When, tentatively, he unhooked one skate and stepped forward, it was not from the prodding; it was simply that he felt too ridiculous hanging upside down and doing nothing. So he took another step away from the platform, and he was looking down into the pit.

It was maybe twenty feet deep, and the bottom was bristling with long, cruel spikes.

"This is stupid," Myron announced. "If I fall in, I won't even die. It'll just hurt a lot."

"We have in our employ," Sukumarika said from the platform, "an immortal vole who will come while you are pinned by spikes and eat your jugular."

The young man began to advance again, more slowly now. Myron tried sidestepping, to circle around him, perhaps, and reach the far platform. He brandished his stick, he hoped threateningly, although waving it affected his balance, and he almost went over backwards again.

"What," said Myron, "has a hundred eyes but cannot see?"

"A potato," said Sukumarika.

"What," said Myron, "is a vole?"

"A field mouse," said Sukumarika.

Myron groaned. He'd thought he'd catch her with that one. The young man came closer, ring by ring. Myron realized he'd need to do something clever, or he was going to die. Or if he couldn't do something clever, he should at least do something different.

"Try this one. Off to see—"

"Stop riddling, Myron," Sukumarika shouted from behind him. "It doesn't matter if you stump me now. It's too late; the riddling is over."

"I'm not talking to you, lady." In his fear and adrenaline, he could not remember her name. "I'm talking to this guy." He pointed his stick at the young man, who batted it away with his own. They were close enough that their staves could touch. "Hey you, you never bested me in a riddle contest. So riddle me this:

> Off to see what I could find
> Through heather and hollow I roam;
> All that I found I left behind,
> What I found not, I brought home."

The young man was busy twirling his staff around in a complicated and frankly intimidating pattern.

"Hey, I'm talking to you," Myron called. "'All that I found I left behind, what I found not I brought home.' What is it?"

The other stopped. "Wait. Say it again," he said.

Myron repeated the rhyme, while stepping forward a ring.

"'What I found not I brought home,'" the young man muttered to himself. "I know I know this one."

Myron then wrapped his legs around each other, such that both feet were in the same ring, facing different ways.

"Oh, I know! Ticks! The answer is ticks."

But holding his stick like a baseball bat, Myron hit the fellow in the shins. A scraping noise, and the man's boots slid back, free of the rings, and he fell through the air. Myron looked away before he hit the spikes. There was no sound. Slowly and very carefully, Myron turned back to the platform. Those same men helped him down. His heart was beating very fast, and he was more terrified than he cared to let on.

The men began to untie Myron's boots. Sukumarika stood in front of him, her lips pursed with displeasure. "I killed him," Myron said. His eyes were tearing up.

Sukumarika silently pointed behind him. Myron looked over his shoulder and saw that the man he had fought was caught in a net that had sprung up, halfway down the pit and well above the spikes. He was clambering across the net like a spider.

Myron was relieved. "Will you tell me where Arthur is?" he asked.

"We don't have to tell you anything. You're lucky to be alive." She was walking him back to the elevator.

"Will you tell me why I'm a dead branch?"

"Like the Illuminati?"

"Yeah, like the Illuminati."

They walked down one flight of stairs and up another flight of stairs, over a catwalk (below, men in white coats could be seen carving with lasers enormous gems), and through a room shaped like a natural cavern, along which flowed sluggishly a stream of what appeared to be honey.

"You're a dead branch," Sukumarika said at last, as they reached a dead end to the corridor, "because your original purpose no longer applies. The Illuminati were formed to stop World War One. This was long before most people could have thought World War One was coming, or even possible, this was the eighteenth century, but the Illuminati had acquired through their parent organization, the Freemasons, certain documents, and they were able to extrapolate that a great war would come and end civilization as we knew it. So, for more than a hundred years, they tried meddling in world affairs, on every level. They started revolutions, and they suppressed revolutions. They signed treaties, and they broke treaties. And then, after all that labor and skullduggery, World War One happened anyway, and ended civilization as we knew it, and then what were the Illuminati to do? They still exist, and they're major property holders in some cities, such as Munich, but there's no reason for them to be around. They're a dead branch, withered and sere, but still attached to the trunk. They're jokes, frankly. Look at the hats they wear! The Nine Unknown Men, and the members of their subsidiaries and affiliates, would never wear such hats!"

"Okay, but why am I a dead branch?"

"I don't mean to be cruel. There was a time when primitive men worshiped totem animals, and then it was needful for some to be halfway between man and animal, with a foot in both worlds."

"Most have four feet, not two," Myron objected, but even he knew he was picking at nits.

"One by one, peoples dragged themselves up from this animism, embracing newer religions. Under the tutelage of the many forms of Hinduism, the Abrahamic religions, Buddhism, Zoroastrianism, or what have you, people abandoned the old ways. With the exception of a few tribes, the animal gods have been forgotten, and these tribes will not last long as they are. And yet you live on. The world has outgrown you, as it has outgrown the Illuminati. The civilization they were formed to preserve, one of progress and innovation, noblesse oblige and grand narratives, no longer exists. And the world you existed for has been dead much longer than that." She fiddled with her earring, and a door hissed open in the dead-end wall. She pushed Myron inside, not ungently. "I guess you could go look for an animist, or maybe even a stoned neopagan. But, really, you have no purpose. Sorry." She handed Myron the garbage bag he'd been carrying; it was more full than before; the door slid shut and all was black.

"You cheated," a voice said, there in the darkness.

Myron's ears were popping, so he had trouble hearing things. "What?" he said.

"You cheated, and I'm going to remember this. I'd watch your back if I were you."

The door opened into the familiar lobby, and Myron could see, in the dim fluorescent light that spilled in, that there in the elevator with him was the young man he had fought.

Myron stepped backwards out of the elevator. "I apologize," he said as the door closed. The young man was saying something, too, but Myron missed it, his voice was so low and ominous.

And then once again the wall was blank.

"Careful of the plant," said the man behind the desk. He still had the accent.

Myron looked around. The floor-waxing machine stood unattended against a wall. The floor shone slickly, and it was cold against Myron's bare feet.

"Did I tell any more lies?" Myron asked.

"I don't think so you did."

"But they told a lie to me. They said I would fall on the spikes, and you know what? There was a net. So they lied about that." Myron turned and walked out the door. As he did, he heard faintly behind him the man saying:

"Why are you sure we would spring the net for you?"

3.

Myron was hardly out the door when the janitor he had seen polishing the floor earlier slipped out of a doorway and fell in step behind him. "Hey, Jackson. Remember me?" he said.

"Sure," Myron said, confused.

"No, I mean, *remember me?*" And he tipped his painter's cap back, revealing the face of the man Myron had met in the library.

"Hey!" Myron said, and then turned to run. He took one step and bumped into the man with the battered fedora and seersucker suit he'd gotten bum directions from. The man was very tall, although old and a little stooped.

"Don't get in a lather, fella, we're on your side," the fedora said. "Come on, let's ankle." *Ankle* meant *walk*. Each man grabbed one of Myron's arms, and dragged him across a street and down a block to a set of benches. On one bench were two other old men, a chessboard between them. They were wearing straw hats and had canes.

"Are you the Illuminati?" Myron asked.

The two men dragging him were rather out of breath, but one of the chess players said, "Pipe the professor here! You really know your onions."

"They said you always wore hats. They said it was ridiculous," Myron said.

The fake janitor let go of Myron's arm, and unzipped his coveralls. Underneath he was wearing the same painted tie. "It's just like them, you'll see, to take every opportunity to get their little digs in. They think they're so smart for going bareheaded." He wiggled the tie.

Myron was looking around for an avenue of escape. Surely he could run faster than any of these four. "What does it matter?" he asked.

"It's true, if you summon the demon Asmodeus while

wearing a hat, he can possess your body. But that's screwy! How often do you summon Asmodeus? And if I were going to, I'd simply *remove my topper.* It's not a big deal."

The chess player moved a bishop. "I can't say I care for the Unknown Men," he said.

"I don't like them, either," Myron said. "They said I was a dead branch, when really I'm more like the chosen one."

All four men threw their hands in the air in disgust. "Faugh! The dead-branch theory! What else did they say?"

"They said you failed to prevent World War One."

"We put it off for a hundred years. If your doctor keeps you alive for a century and then you die, do you call this man a failure?"

"I guess not," Myron said.

The janitor, A. Weishaupt, if that was indeed his real name, put his arm on Myron's shoulder. "Old boy, you can't trust those saps. They're stuck in their antiquated ways, and their forbidden rituals. We just want to help you."

"I sometimes think no one wants to help me," Myron said.

"Well, at the very least, we're not deliberately trying to hurt you. You're the most interesting thing we've seen in years, Jackson. We might be able to help, you know, if you let us know what you want. You didn't mention what you wanted when you were in the lobby."

"I just want to find my parents and have no one trying to kill me," Myron said.

The Illuminati murmured appreciatively. "If someone's

trying to kill you, it can be—mate." The chess players looked up from their game. "It can be a real pill to prevent. The Lord knows we've failed a time or two. Archduke Ferdinand, of course."

"Prince Rudolf at Mayerling," another said.

"Yes, and Robespierre."

"John Keats."

"General Gordon."

"Caroline of Brunswick."

"Alex Raymond."

"Nietzsche."

"But the point is," A. Weishaupt, if that was indeed his real name, interrupted, "that we have succeeded far more often then we have failed."

"Jean Jaurès."

"Hush! Experience, old boy, has taught us that the best way to avoid being killed is to go on the offensive. With our help, you will simply have to take your assailant out before he has a chance to futz you up."

"With your help?"

"Knowledge is power, fella," one of the chess players said. "And we have the knowledge. The history you have learned of, the history of Washington, of Edison and Churchill, is but a tiny spring welling up from the vast underground stream. Madame Blavatsky, Jack the Ripper, and William Henry Ireland didn't get their portraits hung in your history class, but it is their knowledge that flows underground, enriching the soil above."

"And you," Myron said, "have this knowledge?"

"Only a small part, but we know who knows more. This is an entire new world you're moving into, fella, and we can be your guides. What other hope do you have?"

"Well, I do have this doomsday device."

A hush fell over the four men. Very slowly, and with deliberate nonchalance, one said, "Did you say a doomsday device?"

"Yeah, I've got it right here." Myron rooted around in the bag, which he now noticed contained his old street clothes, laundered and folded, plus sneakers—and came out with the cylinder. Its duct tape was still in place. "I don't even know how to open it, though," he said with a fake, dismissive laugh. He began to put it back in the bag.

There was a snapping sound, and the fedora held in front of him a switchblade knife. He flipped it around, catching the blade, and handed it pearl-handle first to Myron. Myron felt awkward. He hadn't really intended to open the package, but it felt like everyone expected him to, and he was too embarrassed to stop what he'd accidentally started.

"I don't know . . ." was the best he could get out.

Do you really think, everyone's eyes seemed to be saying, *you should be carrying around something called a doomsday device and not know exactly what it is?*

The silent argument was persuasive. In absolute stillness, except for the cars passing by, some distant sirens, and the cacophony of the Manhattan crowds, Myron sawed clumsily at the tape. With a little help from his teeth, he managed to cut the top off the cylinder. It was just a cardboard tube under all that tape, the kind inside a roll of wrapping paper. Inside was something wrapped in many layers of tinfoil. He gingerly probed the tinfoil, spreading it out at the top. It extended over the edges of the cylinder like the petals of a flower.

Suddenly the back of Myron's neck erupted in goose flesh. He'd never felt anything quite like this before. He looked over both shoulders, but there was no one suspicious around except some toothless junkies, a pair of blind and deaf drag queens arguing into each other's hands, and a homeless man who had built a three-story castle out of refrigerator boxes. Myron began to feel dizzy. "Is your name really A. Weishaupt?" he said, groggily.

"Myron, you're killing me."

"I don't even know your name."

"My name is Fred Meyers. What's wrong with you?"

"I think I've been drugged. Did you drug me?"

The Illuminati rolled up their sleeves and shook their fists. "The Nine Unknown Men!" they cried. "They must've done this to you!"

"The cads!" one added.

Very slowly, "No, maybe I'm not drugged, maybe it's something else," Myron said. Just then a moose came thundering down the avenue. Cars swerved onto the sidewalk, and people were screaming in its wake. It charged right up to Myron, who dropped the tube. The moose turned into a wild-haired naked man, and he caught it before it hit the ground.

"By the deer on Mora's brow!" the moose-man exclaimed through his long blond beard. "What the de'il is that thing?" He was stuffing, as he spoke, the tinfoil back into place.

"Excuse me," said Fred Meyers. In his hand was a small pistol. "A silver bullet is in the chamber. I suggest you drop the doomsday device."

"You daft son of a whore, do you ken how foul this smells? Silver bullets are naught but a nuisance, and if I cared two pins for your device I'd gore you afore your finger half crooked." He had a strong accent. *Ye daft soon o' a hewer.*

"You have stated your opinion, but the fact of the gun remains," said Fred Meyers. And they all stood there.

"'Tis frightful cold," said the moose-man, who was, after all, completely naked. His hair was so long, it would have come down to his thighs had it not been sticking out in every direction. And to Myron, he said, "These'll be friends of yours?"

"Maybe," said Myron.

Then: With a whistling sound, a disk, like a Frisbee, cut through the air. It passed by fedora's head, slicing a strip off the brim of his hat before embedding itself with a *thock* in the bench. Immediately Fred Meyers spun around, but a second disk cut into his gun, and he dropped it. His hand was scattered and bleeding.

"Get aboard," the moose-man said to Myron, and

dropped the tube. Myron half expected it to explode when it hit the ground, but nothing of the sort happened; it just struck the pavement and rolled six inches, brought up short by a kneeling moose. The Illuminati were scrambling for cover. From across the street was running the young man Myron had fought upside down. In his hand was a long dagger, and his eyes were blazing. He was screaming, and it was hard to catch, but it sounded something like, "I'm good enough to give you a head start, and you stop and talk to the janitor?" The rest was obscenity.

One of the Illuminati tugged on his cane, and out slid a long blade. "Call the Rosicrucians!" he cried. "Call the Knights of Columbus!"

Myron grabbed the doomsday device and jumped on the moose's back. The moose unwound its legs and began to run. Myron looked over his shoulder and saw the young man was chasing him down the sidewalk, slowly losing ground. Then, when he was a block behind, he fell over and disappeared from sight. There was the sound of gunfire. But the moose kept on running. Myron held on tight as it moved across the jammed traffic. It leapt onto a car hood, caving it in, and ran faster and faster over sidewalk and street. Myron was so high up, he was looking down on the pedestrians scattering before him. Soon they reached a tunnel, part of which was blocked off by orange cones; the moose ran through the cones, through the echoing of the tunnel, and out into more city streets on the other side. There were sirens, and the sound of a policeman's voice through a bullhorn. Myron closed his eyes, but he remembered falling out of the truck, and he held on as tight as he could. After what seemed forever, the moose stopped in some woods. He shook Myron onto the ground, and then he was a naked man again.

He said to call him Spenser. He said Myron owed him a set of clothes and some cheese.

V

Flodden Field

They said they would rather be outlaws a year in Sherwood Forest than President of the United States forever.

Mark Twain, *The Adventures of Tom Sawyer*

I.

Upstate New York is cold and overcast in November. There in the woods, the trees were bare, and the leaves crunched beneath their feet.

"See, these all look like dead branches, but in the spring they'll be leafy again," Myron said.

Spenser said, "I have no idea what you're talking about."

"Well, I don't know if you knew this about me—"

"I'm turning back into an elk before I freeze. Hurry up and build the shelter."

Spenser called a moose an elk. He called an elk a wapiti. When he got angry, he started to develop that accent. It took a while, but Myron had managed to summon the accent from him several times over the last day and a half, which had mostly been spent on the move, anyway, Myron riding on mooseback and heading north. There had been a brief stop at a gas station for supplies, where Myron had bought with the last of his money toilet paper, pretzels and a six-pack of orange soda, a T-shirt for Spenser, and toothpaste; but otherwise they had avoided civilization. Now, as night fell, Myron was busy following Spenser's hasty instructions on building a lean-to.

"How come I have to do all the work?" he asked, but the moose just lay there and snorted. Myron knew the answer, anyway. Moose didn't need shelter, but he might. He had put his clothes on under the white pajamas he'd gotten from the Unknown Men, but it was still chilly.

"I've survived plenty of nights in the woods without a lean-to anyway. It's not my fault you've been heading north, and it's been getting colder," Myron said as he jammed leaves into the remaining holes in his frame of sticks. "I could totally survive the night," he said. But that night, which he spent lying beneath the shelter he had made, his head pillowed on the enormous warmth of the moose, was the pleasantest he had spent since leaving home.

In the morning, Spenser, human again, took the toothpaste, squirted some in his mouth, then squirted some more on the toilet paper, and began to polish the bottom of an orange-soda can. He was wearing a T-shirt that said MY PARENTS WENT TO NEW YORK, AND ALL I GOT WAS FETAL ALCOHOL SYNDROME, the only one they'd had in his size.

"Can I have some, too?" Myron asked. "I haven't brushed my teeth in forever."

Spenser spat out the toothpaste. "You don't need to brush your teeth," he said, still polishing. "You can't get cavities." When the toilet paper shredded, he took another piece, and he kept using more toothpaste. But he let Myron have a shot, too, to swish out his mouth. It felt much better afterward, and then they both drank some orange soda.

Myron noticed that the bottom of Spenser's can was as shiny as a mirror. He pointed at it, his mouth still full of soda.

"The sun's finally out this morning, so I can show you. You can use this mirror to start a fire."

(Swallowing.) "Why do I need a fire? I was really warm last night."

"You'll need a fire to cook food, and I might not always be here. Lookit." Spenser held the can's polished bottom up to the sun, and moved a dry leaf back and forth in front of it. The parabolic mirror of the curved bottom of the can focused the sun's rays on a point, and when he found that point he held the leaf there until it burst into flames.

Myron screamed. But it was mostly, you know, joy and wonder.

Spenser went over the process again, the polishing, the focal point, and the importance of building up a base of tinder to burn, to which you could add first small twigs and then larger branches. Myron was well versed in the literature of Jack London, so he knew most of this, the part that came after the soda can. "So that's what the toilet paper's for," he said.

"No, the toilet paper is for you. You'll thank me for that one."

Spenser had brought with him to New York a backpack full of supplies, but he had left it all behind when he suddenly moosed in downtown Manhattan. The clothes he had been wearing had, of course, been torn to shreds.

"I don't know what's in that tube," he said—not the toothpaste tube, the duct-taped cylinder—"but it smells terrible. I could smell it from a mile away, and I mean that literally. I was crosstown in Alphabet City."

"It's a doomsday device," Myron said.

"Well, keep it in the tinfoil if you have to keep it at all. If I can smell it, someone else can smell it, and you dinna want to attract attention out here."

Spenser, it turned out, more than anything didn't want to attract attention. He spent most of his time alone in the woods, as moose or man, and only occasionally ventured into the "human lands." What he called supplies were obtainable at any number of small towns, but only in New York did he have a connection to obtain his cheese.

"Young" cheese, cheese that has not been aged, is filled with bacteria. It is a health hazard. It is therefore illegal to sell it in the United States, unless it has been made with pasteurized milk. But to young-cheese aficionados, the pasteurization process ruins the flavor. Spenser was, he would assure Myron, a man or moose of simple tastes, but he did love his cheese, and he loved it unaged, bacterial, stench-ridden, and untainted by pasteurization.

It was for the sake of cheese that Spenser made an annual pilgrimage to New York, where a certain cheese shop, unnamed here, permitted the cognoscenti into a backroom stocked with forbidden cheese smuggled from Europe.

"I was lucky you picked that day to go in," Myron said.

"See what you think is lucky when the snow starts to fall. And as soon as you opened the tinfoil, everyone in New York knew what was going on. There was no question someone was going to show up, the only question was who was going to get there first."

"Well, I'm lucky it wasn't a squirrel or something," Myron said. But Spenser wouldn't listen to anything of the sort. He packed up the toothpaste and the toilet paper and the cans and the T-shirt into a plastic bag. There were no pretzels left.

"You should throw it in the river," Spenser said, and then turned into a moose, so there could be no discussion or rebuttal. Myron rode on his back, and the bag hung on an antler. The tube Myron carried in one chilly hand.

Day after day they moved north. Myron got better, or at least more efficient, at building the lean-to. He learned how to find two trees with low branches close enough that he could stretch a stick between them. He'd lean other sticks against this crosspiece, then weave twigs and leaves among them, and it was here that he got much faster, as he figured out just how loosely he could construct the thing without letting too much wind, or the rain, through. When the sun came out from behind the ever-present clouds, he built fires.

And Spenser showed him the rudiments of building snares, of tracking game, of digging up edible roots, and, as the weather grew colder, how to find the dens of hibernating rodents or bats, and scoop them out before they had a chance to wake. Bats in winter, Myron found, were as cold as death, their hearts beating too feebly to feel.

"These are good eating," Spenser said, roasting one over the fire. But they weren't really good eating.

At night (Myron may have been inspired by a scene in *Huckleberry Finn* to contrive the scenario) they lay around the fire and looked up at the stars, and Spenser taught him their names, and how to use them to find directions. But that only happened on the rare nights that were not overcast. Other times Myron pillowed his head against a moose and told him of his adventures, with Mr. Rodriguez and Gloria and the Unknown Men. Only a twitching ear, every few minutes, indicated that the moose had not yet fallen asleep.

"And it turned out that I was some kind of chosen one," Myron said. This was his favorite part. He wondered what his parents would think, to know he was a messianic figure, and hoped they would not be disappointed that he was not the one they'd been waiting for.

Next morning, Spenser, as he boiled up some roots in a soda-can half, said, "That stuff you mentioned about being the chosen one. That stuff is shite." But Myron didn't worry about it. He wasn't sure how smart Spenser was. The man believed all sorts of strange things. He believed mice were spontaneously generated from riverbanks, and maggots from cheese. He had to admit he had not seen cheese give birth to maggots for many years, but Myron facetiously suggested it might have something to do with pasteurization.

"It might at that," Spenser said.

"This sounds like a good argument for pasteurized cheese," Myron began, but Spenser would have none of that. And when Myron tried to persuade him that cheese did not create maggots ex nihilo, but rather harbored eggs laid there by flies, Spenser told him not to doubt the evidence of his senses for a whole bunch of modern superstitions. And Myron's senses told him rather incontrovertibly that he was chosen.

Later, around Albany, Spenser dug up one of his caches: soap, spare clothing (too large for Myron) including pants at last, gloves, crunchy granola, and some cookware, all wrapped tightly in a tarp. Around Schenectady the snow began in earnest.

"Do we wait out the winter here?" Myron asked. He had caked his lean-to with snow, and built snow walls and a grand snow entrance, complete with snow pillars and a snow guardsman, who was deforming in the heat of the campfire. But Spenser was a moose again, and made no answer until the next day, crouched over the embers.

"We can wait, or we can move on, and it doesn't much matter which." He was still brooding over his cheese, Myron thought.

"But where are we going?"

Spenser stroked his long beard, a nervous habit Myron

had started imitating with his bare, scarred chin. "Do you mean where are we going right now, or where are we going in the long term?"

"I mean in the end," Myron said.

"You've got to understand that 'in the end' is the wrong way to think. That's how humans think, because they end up in the ground. But I've been at this a long time, and there hasn't been any 'in the end' yet."

"Sure, but we can't spend forever in the woods."

"That's what I'm trying to make you understand. You might want to think about living forever in the woods."

Myron was so shocked by the idea that he slipped and fell in the snow. He was wearing a thick wool shirt long enough on him to pass as a nightgown. The sleeves had been cut in half. "Why would I want to spend forever in the woods?" he asked, looking up from the ground at the bare branches and the massed clouds. As he spoke, his breath billowed up opaque above him.

"You've got the lion trying to kill you, by your own admission, and kill you for real," Spenser said. "And then all sorts of other people, from these secret societies, are after you. They control everything except the wilderness out here, and they're always up to no good."

"The Illuminati weren't up to no good. They delayed World War One for a hundred years."

"Sure, they delayed it just long enough, long enough for humans to invent new weapons to make the war really bad and really long. It's hardly something to be proud of. If they haven't done any harm since then, it's because they're jokes now. All they do is name-drop a lot. You don't want to get involved with them anyway, trust me. You're better off out here."

"I was kind of under the impression, frankly, that I should be doing something."

"Myron, if there was something you could do, maybe I would agree with you. But you're thinking like a human again. You think you can do something and then everything's going to be okay for the rest of your life. Except there is no rest of your life. It's just going to keep going and going, and even if you achieve something now, what then? Will you just want to do something else? Because whatever you want to do is going to be blocked, or perverted, or manipulated by the Unknown Men and the Rosicrucians and the Gnomes of Zurich."

"Who are the Rosicrucians? I keep hearing their name."

Spenser stood up, and his accent was back. "Are ye listening, lad? These are the six or seven societies that rule the earth, and at least one of them's wroth at ye!" *Ane o' tham's wroth at ye* it sounded like. "Every year they move civilization a little farther out into the woodlands and the, sure, and the glens, and every year it gets harder to find a place they are not monitoring. All we can do is wait for them, and when we are hiding in the last swatch of tall grass, and they are mowing it down, we'll know that we will be slaves forever. All we could do was delay the inevitable."

"Like the Illuminati."

"If you like. But maybe they'll end up killing each other. Maybe all of them will end up killing each other, and then they'll leave us alone."

"Is that what you want, just to be left alone?"

"Why do you think I spend all my time in the woods?"

Myron waved his arms in frustration. "I thought you lived out here because you loved nature and Mother Earth and stuff."

"Mother Earth? Who taught you to talk that way? Earth is no more your mother than the land is your father. There is nothing but a vast, uncaring emptiness."

"I don't think I'm supposed to believe in stuff like that."

"What you're supposed to believe in doesn't matter much."

"But why, then—why did you bother picking me up?"

"You looked like you needed help. Time will tell if I made a mistake or not." He stood up. "Put snow on the embers, we should get moving."

"Where?" Myron asked, but he got on mooseback anyway, and was off.

2.

The days blended together into an endless panorama of ice fishing, snow forts, and winterberries. Spenser told Myron, at times, stories from the inexhaustible store of his life. He had been an elk, as he styled it, in what is now Scotland, for millennia, occasionally traveling south through Britain or swimming, for variety, to Ireland. It was there he learned, from the Tuatha dé Dannan who ruled the island at the time, that he could change into a human. As a human he watched Stonehenge built. As a human he saw exiles from a land they called Egypt beach in Ireland and found the new ruling dynasty—and this was the first he had heard of lands beyond the islands he knew. As a human he fought alongside Finn mac Cumail and his warrior band, across Great Britain, Ireland, and the Isle of Man. But mostly, to escape from what he characterized to Myron as "incessant human sacrifice," he returned to the uninhabited wilds of Scotland.

It was there that the Roman general Agricola found him, while marching the length of Britain, driving the natives in their war chariots before his unconquerable might. Agricola either pressed or accepted the wild man into his legion. His beard was shaved, for the first time ever, and he learned to drill with a long spear. Rome, when he reached there, was certainly impressive, but it didn't take him long to realize that the Romans were not much of an upgrade from the barbarities of the druids. They were just more efficient. Emperor Domitian's hands were stained red with the blood of fellow Romans, and everyone else wallowed in the blood of Rome's neighbors.

Later, in Dacia, on the shores of the Black Sea, Spenser's company (a *century,* he called it) got singled out for cowardice, and was scheduled for a *decimation*—a process by which the company was divided into groups of ten, and each group drew lots; the one who drew the bad lot was supposed to get bludgeoned to death by the other nine. Spenser didn't draw the bad lot, but he got up and left anyway. "Say it was me, say you beat me to a pudding," he told the other nine in bad Latin. It was one thing to kill Dacians, which was just the kind of thing you did back then, but he balked at turning on his own comrades. An elk ran into the woods.

"The Romans make desolation and call it peace," General Agricola's grandson wrote. For a century, the borders of Rome were an orgy of bloodshed, after which the reign of the "five good emperors" ended, and things, predictably, got much, much worse.

Anyone's life story takes a long time in the telling, and a story that spans several hundred lifetimes much longer. Spenser jumped around a lot, and focused on the stuff Myron would like, the stuff found in his adventure novels. Pirates and crusaders and frontiersmen; bravery and bloodshed. But in Spenser's accounts, every act of bravery was, ultimately, futile, every heroic action a waste of time, and every story an incipient tragedy. The bloodshed, not the bravery, was the real point of his stories.

The ancient Celts were bound, each individual was bound, by a complicated series of *geasa,* or taboos. In this way, Munremar son of Gerrchenn (with whom Spenser was, two thousand years ago, acquainted) was placed under *geis* not to cut his beard until he had slain the witch woman Cailleach Beara; later he learned that Cailleach Beara was under a *geis* such that she could not be killed except by a bare-faced man. And so Munremar, to resolve this contradiction, held his head in the fire until the beard burned away, and only then, with scarred and bubbling face, was he able to slay the witch. In one sense, this was an action of the most selfless devotion to a cause. But the way Spenser told the story, it became a tale of how one man ruined his face and his health in order to murder a helpless crazy woman.

Myron told stories, too, but they were mainly stories from books he had read. He did the plot of *Treasure Island* over three nights, and he fancied that Spenser was held in rapt attention by the production. Or he went over again and again the strange events of the last few months, looking for clues. Spenser hated and feared the Nine Unknown Men, but he finally revealed, as they sat around the campfire one night, that he had once had occasion to ask them a riddle himself. He had asked, "What animal is it that hath a tail between its eyen?"

"What are eyen?" Myron said.

"It's an old way of making something plural, like *children* or *brethren*. It means *eyes*."

"Oh. Why don't you talk old-fashioned like that more often, if you're so old?"

"You learn to adapt to that kind of thing. If I spoke old-fashioned, you wouldn't be able to understand a word."

"I could understand," said Myron, who had read Walter Scott. "I know all those *thees* and *thous* and things."

Spenser looked grim. "You still don't really understand

what all this means. Have you ever met anyone who's only a hundred and fifty or two hundred years old?"

Myron conceded he had not.

"There are a few around, necromancers and alchemists mainly. And they're always stuck in a world that ended a century ago. I mean, they can't adapt to anything modern. They hate automobiles and telephones, they flip out in the motion pictures, and in the end they retreat more and more into the trappings of their childhoods—panopticons and hornbooks or whatever. But my childhood was spent among elks. The only things around were trees and hills. Forget automobiles, I had to get used to walking on two legs, and then wearing pants, eating with my hands, and then eating with a knife. Old-fashioned talk? I can barely remember the human language I first learned, but . . . it was something like . . ." And here he produced a few tongue-twisting sentences so bleak and alien that Myron dropped the stick he was holding. The bat on the end of it landed in the fire, and its wing membranes went up like tissue paper. Myron scrambled to save dinner, and only later, as he was getting ready to go to sleep, did he ask Spenser what the terrifying sentences were.

Spenser was still stirring the fire up. "An invocation to the fourteen chthonic gods of Hatheg-Kla," he said.

"Fourteen? Why fourteen?" asked Myron.

After a long pause, Spenser said, "Because the fifteenth died."

Myron thought this all sounded so cool. "That thing you said, can you," he asked, "say it again?"

Spenser could not help but smile as out of the terrifying and oppressive darkness behind the campfire he intoned, "Pax sax sarax . . ."

3.

One morning Myron woke up with a start. Spenser was missing. He stumbled out of the lean-to and saw two moose; one was obviously Spenser, the other had no antlers. Myron made a guess about what was up and ducked back into the lean-to. Later, when Spenser was making breakfast, Myron quizzed him about it. "Was that a lady moose?" he asked.

"What? No, he was male."

"Then how come he had no antlers?"

"Moose shed their antlers for the winter."

"Oh yeah?" Myron crowed. "Then how come you still have antlers?"

"I travel around too much some years, it interferes with the rhythms. They'll fall off sooner or later." He looked worried, or perhaps guilty and guarded about something.

But Myron didn't believe him. Every once in a while, as he rode that day, he'd tweak Spenser about having a girlfriend, until Spenser bucked him off, onto and through the thin ice of a frozen pond. They spent the rest of the day drying Myron out by a fire. Spenser fretted about the delay and tried to look grim-faced, but when he saw Myron's hair, wetted and then frozen onto crazy shapes, he couldn't help smiling.

Myron glowered at him, and spread in front of the fire his meager possessions. The cardboard tube he'd been carrying was sodden through the tape, and he went to open it, but suddenly Spenser kicked it out of his hands.

"Lene larbar, longeur baith lowsy in lisk and lonye!" Spenser shouted, his Scotch accent indecipherable.

"Are you insane?" Myron shouted back. "That's a doomsday device!"

"Are ye insane to open such a thing? Dinna ye ever open that; there be wraiths in the wood."

"What does that mean?"

"All right, all right," Spenser said. "The moose I saw, he says they're something in the forest, something big and terrifying he's no seen here before."

"Moose can talk?"

"Of course they cannae talk, but ye can tell. Ye can smell their fear. There's something out there, and two shillings say it means ye nae guid." *No good,* he meant. The word *lion* neither one mentioned, but the lion was out there, somewhere. Myron hoped that lions hated snow.

They dried the cardboard tube out as well as they could without opening it. It came out warped and stained. And then they traveled for two days straight, like fugitives. Afterward, the moose pretended nothing was different, but as he walked he moved his giant head, always, back and forth. At times he would stand stock-still and listen. Myron held his breath. The branchings of the sensitive antlers conducted sound very well, and a moose in full display has hearing far better than a human's.

These were the days of fear. Every day Spenser combed the surrounding countryside for sinister tracks, but there were only the usual things: rabbits, deer, hikers. Once Myron caught a glimpse of a bald eagle gliding directly overhead, there in the dead of winter.

"I've never seen one of those before," Myron said, in awe.

"We've got to get a bow," Spenser said, his eyes narrowing suspiciously.

They bought one. Spenser wove Myron a kind of mask out of pliant branches, then stuck small deer antlers he'd dug up in it, and Myron made a sign out of garbage that read MOOSE RIDES: $5. They spent several days by the highway, and took a trip to town and spent all the money at a pawnshop on a children's compound bow and several hunting arrows. They also got a decent meal and a sleeping bag that could roll up into a small pouch; which was the better purchase, as the eagle never returned. But Spenser taught Myron to shoot, and bade him keep the bow, and an arrow with a broad, jagged head, ever ready.

For there was danger in the forest. Previously, they had been spending a few days at one campsite, collecting enough food that they could march, or moose-ride, for a couple of days without stopping to forage; but now Spenser pushed them to move every day. Snow was all they drank. "It'll get easier in the summer," Spenser said. But Myron feared nothing now, and he was living a life of woodcraft and adventure and having a ball.

"Wait," he said suddenly, "did they guess your riddle?"

"Did who guess my riddle?"

"The Unknown Men. Did they figure out the riddle you gave them?"

"They always figure out the riddles. They have a brazen head that answers all questions."

"Okay. So what animal has a tail between its eyen?"

Spenser said, "It is a cat, when it licketh its arse."

Myron laughed and laughed. If only, he thought, it hadn't been so freezing cold. Also, they ran out of toothpaste.

Spenser's hair had grown so long and wild that Myron taught him how to wrap it around his waist like a belt, after the fashion of old mountain men and explorers he'd read about. Book learning was good for something, at least.

One day, as Myron was untangling some fishing line, Spenser put a hand on his shoulder. Moments later, Myron felt a new prickling sensation. Spenser pulled him up by his shirt and dragged him over, through quite a few burrs and thorns, to a low fork in a dogwood tree. Peering between the two trunks, Myron saw, ambling among some pines, what looked like an enormous armadillo, ten feet long. Its gigantic shell taller than a man looked like a turtle's, and armor plating covered its shaggy forehead and its tail, which was tipped with a spiked club like a morning star. Ponderously it moved, plowing deep furrows in the snow, and it browsed on pine needles.

"So that's what the moose was worried about. But she's harmless. She just doesn't usually come this far north," Spenser said.

"Does it know we're here?" Myron asked.

"Of course, she just doesn't care. She never talks to anyone."

"She must be very lonely," Myron said. He watched until with excruciating slowness the enormous bulk trailed out of sight.

That beast, last of an extinct species, was a relic of the past. But around the campfire, started with their soda-can mirror or, on cloudy days, with a book of matches from a convenience store, Spenser's stories moved closer to the current age and finally entered what he called the Time of Troubles. He circled around the issue for a while before finally plunging into it. All times were times of troubles, after all, but at some point in the seventeenth century, "our people" (immortal lycanthropes, he meant) began to realize how things worked. At best the squirrel may have known for thousands of years that a fox and a beaver passed beneath his trees that were different from other foxes and beavers, and the squirrel may even have known that they were, like him, capable of assuming human form, but it was not until now that immortal lycanthropes pieced together that there was one of us for each species of animal (the idea that animals had species, as scientists use the word today, was still nascent); that we could only be killed by another of our kind; that the presence of another could be perceived from twenty or thirty yards; that only the beasts, as opposed to the birds or the cold and slimy things, were represented. No marsupials, either, and no egg-layers, like the platypus or the spiny echidna. All this we were finally piecing together.

The result was panic. Creatures who for millennia thought they were unique discovered they were only slightly unique; creatures who for millennia thought they knew all five or six similarly special beings now learned there were untold thousands more out there. An orgy of bloodletting followed. The tiger killed the tapir, the onager, the lynx and the leopard, the porcupine, the sloth bear, several monkeys, no one knows how many mice and shrews and hares and hedgehogs, and, in a fight that lasted three days on and off, the Indian elephant. Then he began to travel and killed the badger, the Javan rhinoceros, the wolf, the gnu, the quagga, the snow leopard, the spectacled bear, the impala, the chamois, the raccoon dog, the genet, the eland, the orangutan, and a dozen others, many of which Myron had never heard of. And then he crossed over to the Americas. The porcupine and the badger were dead, but there were still New World porcupines and badgers, many New World monkeys, and strange species that had never known something like a tiger had even existed. The puma went down fighting, and the pronghorn went down running. The two-toed sloth just went down.

But the tiger was not alone by any means. Everyone began to kill whomever he could, for fear that he would himself die. The chipmunk attacked the wildcat's eyes, and the mandrill tore to pieces six kinds of baboon, the chimpanzee, and a pangolin. A general massacre came down upon the bats, strange, liminal birdlike beings hated by all, and the bats were too busy fighting among themselves to realize what was happening (though there were too many kinds of bats, far too many, to make a dent in). The aardvark used her claw-hooves on small or slow creatures until the hyrax bit off her tongue, and, unable to eat, she keeled over from weakness and the jerboa finished her off. But the hyrax had died, too. They were rotten years all around. Everyone who did not become clinically paranoid died. You were either always afraid or you were a goner.

But, after the easy marks and the innocent perished, the survivors, who were tough, or canny, or small, or elusive, eventually settled down. But some, their blood fired by the years of slaughter, turned their attention outward. Those were the days of action, although most of the actions were vain and futile, of course. The flying squirrel murdered Friedrich Nietzsche in the madhouse. The babirusa somehow contrived to set off the volcanic explosion of Krakatoa. The gorilla assassinated Prime Minister Antonio Cánovas, and her friend the Barbary ape conspired, tried, and failed to assassinate Napoleon III; was sentenced to death; would not die; and so he was sent to Devil's Island, from which he predictably escaped, for no such island can long hold a Barbary ape. "I knew him well," Spenser said. "He went on and fought in the Civil War, for the Union, under the name Charles DeRudio, and later survived the battle of Little Big Horn, too, always running rashly and some would say nobly into danger, to no result. He was killed by the wolverine."

"But you know Gloria?" Myron asked.

"Who?"

"The gorilla."

"Oh, sure, sure. She came to Scotland in the reign of good King James the Fourth, actually, which is where I met her. She only spoke French, I remember. Not long after that, the French king forced James to invade England, and he died, with the flower of Scottish gentility, near Flodden Field; and Scotland never recovered."

Myron wasn't sure if he believed this, that Gloria had gone to Scotland in the sixteenth century or that she had been an assassin in Spain in the nineteenth. He wasn't sure in general what to believe. It didn't help that whatever his subject, Spenser returned to the basic idea that no matter what monumental deeds of bravery or chivalry he witnessed, these only affected things in the short term, and the short term was precisely what should not affect him, or Myron, at all. Even the improvements—like when the Scottish kings, at long last, stopped burning witches—were cosmetic, unimportant when compared to the ways in which life, and all people, kept getting worse. The vast forests of Europe had been mowed down to make room for idiots in plaid pants and sandals, and now the vast forests of America were going, too, to make room for idiots in Bermuda shorts and Nikes. Year after year people became weaker and stupider and more inured to mediocrity. All under the direction of obscure and sinister secret societies. Sometimes their motivation was naked lust for power; sometimes it was ineffable; sometimes it seemed like a personal vendetta against Spenser, and when he got to that point, the moose started to sound like a loon.

And one afternoon, while Myron was setting snares, the moose came back from foraging. His head was bleeding, and he had no antlers. He turned back into a human and washed his bloody forehead off before dressing.

"Are you all right?" Myron asked.

"A headache, nothing more. It should've happened months ago, but I'm frequently off schedule."

"But you'll be better now," Myron suggested.

"Sure, sure."

"I mean, this must be a load off your mind."

Spenser didn't suss out the pun for a few eyeblinks, and when he did he threw a snowball at Myron. Rebounding, the snowball struck the snare Myron had just set, and a sapling springing to attention shot a flurry of snow back at Spenser, covering him head to toe. Myron laughed so hard, he almost wet himself.

"Fy, skolderit skyn, thou art bot skyre and skrumple!" Spenser roared, but he was joking, now, too. They both fell down and laughed. Myron was looking forward to warmer weather, but that was all, he realized, he was looking forward to. They were alone in the wide woods, and there was nothing to fear. For the first time in years, in all the years he could remember, he was satisfied.

(Later that day:) Spring comes like a miracle, and the repetition of the miracle has still not cheapened it. There exist many sentimental descriptions of the first bluebird of the spring, or of a crocus, blooming up through the melting snow. Myron, for his part, had pried up and half overturned a hollow log and saw underneath a dark snake, its distended jaw half swallowing a frog. The frog's legs were still kicking. Meanwhile, from the frog's back end, its cloaca to be precise, a long, pale strand of spaghetti was twisting and writhing. It took Myron a moment to realize what was happening. The strand was a parasitic worm, and, as its host was being devoured, it was desperately trying to escape digestion by inching its way into the open air.

"That is the most disgusting thing I have ever seen," Myron said.

Spenser came and looked over his shoulder. "You know what that means," he said.

Myron was temporarily terrified that the scene was a revolting allegory he would have to determine the meaning of. But instead, Spenser said, "They're not hibernating. It means spring has come."

It was not at that moment, it was the next morning, or possibly the morning after that it happened. Myron had broken camp and packed everything they had—the bedding, extra clothes, the doomsday device, the archery equipment, and sundries like fishhooks and the soda-can mirror—into duffle bags, and he stood there, next to the moose, unsure of where to put them. Always before he had hung them on the antlers. The moose was pacing, impatient to leave. He swung his great head toward Myron.

Myron said, "I just don't know where to put—"

And then there was a crashing in the forest. Something burst through a bush, sending up an enormous spray of snow, and dimly through that spray Myron could see the figure of a bear, brown and enormous, bringing a paw down on Spenser's neck. Spenser went over with a great crash, taking a midsize tree down with him. Instantly he sprang to his feet again, and Myron could see the raw red wound where the paw had struck. He leapt forward, butting the bear with his head, but the wounds, where his antlers had been, just tore open. In the haze of another great spray of snow, the bear knocked him down again.

Rising slower now, on his knees, he spent a moment looking back at Myron. His eyes were the saddest things. He jerked his head and pointed with his nose, pointing away. He had to do it twice. As the bear struck again, Myron turned and ran. He dropped everything and bolted for where the trees were densest. The snow was still deep, and his legs moved slowly, as in a dream. He had never gotten boots, he was still in his old sneakers, with just rubber overshoes (ill-fitting, fished from a Dumpster) to protect against the snow; they worked all right when he was treading gingerly, but now scarcely three steps and snow was pouring into his sneakers over the top, and his feet became slippery and numb. Branches whipped against his face, and one caught him and cut him right above the eye. The trickle of blood was first hot and then icy cold in the wind as it ran down his cheek. Leaping over a log, Myron found that on the far side was a steep hill, which he proceeded to tumble down, head over heels. He skidded to a stop against some rocks at the bottom, and when he stood up, he found he was standing on an iced-over stream. His foot immediately broke through, and when he jerked it back, a jagged ice shard sliced through two socks and cut his ankle. The water from the frigid stream had collected in the rubber overshoe, and it was so hard to run in the sodden shoe. He tried to persuade himself that his best chance was to hide, but he knew that was not true; there was no way to hide a trail in the snow. He stood up and headed off again, again for the thick trees where something large would have trouble pushing through. The blood from the cut on his eyebrow had become diverted somehow and now spilled directly into his eye. He tried to wipe it away with one stiff and frozen hand. All the time he imagined he could hear a bear behind him, getting closer. And it was not his imagination, and the bear was there, and with one swipe it knocked him down.

VI

The Shape

"I fear me, Cuthbert, this is far from the spirit in which
   we a while ago agreed that men should go to the
   holy war."
Cuthbert hung his head a little.
"Ay, Father Francis, men; but I am a boy," he said, "and
   after all, boys are fond of adventure for adventure's
   sake."

G. A. Henty, *Winning His Spurs*

I.

Melodrama is my usual, if not necessarily my preferred, idiom, so you can imagine how difficult it was for me not to
falsify the preceding events. How choice it would have been
if, right before poor Spenser perished, he had finally found
the cheese of his dreams! He reaches one hoof gingerly toward the wedge, which is emanating visible stink lines, and
only then does he fall. His last words are poignant, and in-
volve some kind of pun on Edam.

But absolute fidelity to facts, established through exten-
sive interviews of the participants, especially young Myron
in this instance, forbid my coloring of events with my usual
palette. And so it is with no mendacious or even mislead-
ing rhetorical flourish that I draw back the curtain on a
scene in which our hero awakens in a bed in a small round
room, tastefully appointed. The red rays of the sunset stream

through a small circular window. A low bookshelf squats beside the bed, like an incubus preparing to clamber into position. Entering the room are two women. One, moving as quickly and nervously as a chain smoker, is black and has the gangly limbs of a teenager; she stands well under five feet tall, and if she is wearing children's clothing (striped shirt & purple overalls), perhaps this is why. The other is very pale, tall and slender, perhaps thirty, her blond hair cut short and her fashionable gray business skirt cut to the knee. I will go so far as to say that, in the magical and forgiving light of dusk, she is beautiful. Perhaps she looks familiar. It's very cold; Myron's neck is prickling, and this is what has awakened him.

"Well," and it is the taller woman who speaks, as taller people always do, "how are we feeling today?" In the chill, her breath is faintly visible. She bends over above him, her movements slow and languid, and places the back of her hand on Myron's forehead.

All the confusion of the moment is right then swept away by amazement that someone, anyone, is able to touch his face without flinching. And so Myron could only gape, dumbfounded as the woman explained that one of her employees had been some distance from here walking in the woods, collecting mistletoe, and had chanced to come across Myron, bloody and half frozen. As she spoke, silently the teenager, all four and a half feet of her, paced back and forth with a glass of water in each hand. Myron was tucked in tight, the heavy covers up to the chin, but his eyes darted back and forth between the two. He could see on the floor beyond her his bow, the cardboard tube, and a duffle bag that was not his. He could barely bring himself to ask the obvious question.

"Was there," said Myron, "when the guy found me, was there a moose with me?"

"A moose?"

The air on Myron's face was cold, and he realized that the little window was wide open. It opened outward, like a door, on a little hinge. "Not with me, I mean, but back, back where I left my stuff. That stuff over there."

"No. We followed your tracks back to locate the bow and some other things, which we took the liberty of consolidating in a duffle bag. But I can assure you we would have noticed a moose." She smiled, quite a lovely smile, to show she could be ironical, and Myron let out a long billow of breath. The lack of a moose was a relief; no body could mean that Spenser had escaped whatever had attacked them.

The woman was asking, "What's your name?"

"Vladimir Speed," said Myron. "What's yours?"

"This is Florence Agalega, and I am called Mignon Emanuel."

Myron passed out. But it was only for a moment; he woke from the shock of cold water in the face. Florence was reaching out—reaching up, actually—and offering him the remaining glass of water. "Sorry about that," she whispered.

All Myron could think about at the moment was that the offer was absurd, as his arms were both beneath the bed-spread.

"Vladimir," said Mignon Emanuel, smoothing her skirt before she sat on the bed across from Florence. She carefully avoided any wet spots. "Do you mind if I call you Myron? You really are very fortunate we found you."

"Fortunate?" Myron cried, coming to himself. At which point he tried to throw back the covers and leap out of bed, but he found that he was securely pinned under the heavy blankets. There had been very little give before, and now Mignon Emanuel was sitting on one side of him, Florence leaning on the bedspread on the other side. Neither one could have weighed much, but Myron had no leverage and, to be frank, was not very strong at all. But he wriggled back and forth desperately. He remembered the frog's parasitic worm, and, like that worm, he would not give up.

"And we are similarly fortunate to have found you. For you are instrumental to our plan."

"Your plan to kill me!" he shrieked.

"Killing you would be counterproductive, not to mention impolite to a guest."

"You're not fooling me, I saw you in the car. You work for Mr. Bigshot."

"For—for whom?" Mignon Emanuel's puzzlement seemed so genuine that Myron stopped his writhing. Could he have the situation all wrong?

"Mr. Bigshot," he said. "You know, the lion."

"You mean Marcus?" She laughed, I am compelled to say musically. I've heard it, and it really is a charming laugh. "Our association has been terminated, I'm sorry to say. What did you call him again?"

"Mr. Bigshot? Isn't that his name? I mean, what he goes by?"

"Heavens no! Where did you get that idea?"

"That's what Gloria called him. And Arthur and Alice."

"Oh, those characters! They were having a little fun at his expense, I suppose. Mr. Bigshot!" Mignon Emanuel reached across Myron, taking the glass of water from Florence's hand. For a moment Myron could see, in the buckling of her blouse's collar, a nasty purple bruise on her shoulder. She then stood up. Every move was very slow and deliberate, either through general habit or to avoid spilling the water. With her body off the blankets, Myron managed to work a hand out, and no sooner had he extracted it than Mignon Emanuel slipped the glass into it. Myron had more or less meant to use the free hand to tear the covers off, but, with water in his hand, he realized he was thirsty. He downed the glass in three swallows, and, as he brought his arm down, he found Mignon Emanuel was taking the glass from him and replacing it with a handkerchief.

"Your face will be cold. We wanted you to get some fresh air, but there's still a chill, isn't there? And now you're wet!"

Myron began to dab his wet face with the handkerchief. It felt like what he was supposed to do.

"You don't work for the lion anymore?" he asked.

"I'm afraid our current relationship is more akin to rivalry. Which is indeed why you are instrumental. And you must get out of the habit of saying *the lion*."

"Um. Marcus, then?" Myron said.

"It's terribly imprecise, I am sure you'll find. He is *Panthera leo*."

"He is what?"

"*Panthera leo,* the proper nomenclature for Marcus Lynch. I am *Procyon lotor,* and Florence is *Lemur catta*. Do you know what you are, Myron?"

"I don't know what they call it in Greek, but I think I know what I am"; and Mignon Emanuel chewed her lip and nodded conspiratorially when Myron said, "The chosen one."

2.

A short, stocky redheaded boy, perhaps a little older than Myron but still in freckles, brought some food in later—roast beef on rye and a bowl of applesauce.

He watched Myron eat. "Have you seen the shape?" he asked.

"I have no idea what you're talking about," Myron said between bites.

"Well, I'll give you some advice, if you want to survive in this place. Stay away from Florence."

"Is she dangerous?"

"No, but she's mine. Or she will be, and I don't need any competition."

"I'm not—"

"I know you're not, and I'm not supposed to mention your face, but I know you're not competition. I'm just saying, is all."

"Say, my neck isn't prickling," Myron said. "You're not one of us?"

"Wrong again, you're not one of *us*. Even those guys out there, the infantry, they're not one of us, and you're not even one of them." He left. He hadn't understood, Myron noted, and then he realized: the boy didn't know.

Some time later, when he came back, the boy, whose name, he said with a brisk handshake, was Oliver, gathered the dishes and asked Myron if he was able to stand. After testing out his wobbly legs, Myron said sure, and regretted it when he learned that he was at the top of an endless spiral staircase. The steep stone steps went on and on, and Oliver, supporting Myron on his shoulder, explained briefly that Myron had been stationed at the top of "the east tower," the highest point of the house. "Or the fortress," he corrected himself. Fortress or house, the building was clearly huge, and Myron even on level ground found his weak legs wearying of the walk down galleries peppered with old portraiture, tiny envased tables, and the occasional suit of armor. The Oriental carpets were lush, the walls wood-paneled a dark brown. Through the windows came the morning sun, and the windows were all stained glass, so the walls and even Oliver as he walked appeared lit in a kaleidoscope of colors. Nebulae of dust motes swirled in the colored beams. Nevertheless, the spaces between the windows were dim, and while some of the many recesses were populated by statues, others were populated only by deep shadows. From outside came muffled shouts; it sounded like a lot of people out there, whatever they were doing. Myron hummed nervously to himself.

Finally the two reached a set of enormous double doors bearing a plaque that read M.E. Ignoring the buzzer, Oliver knocked, two brisk raps, and, although the muffled response was impossible to make out, he pushed one door open. Myron, unsure of what to do, put his shoulder to the other door, and was amazed to find how heavy it was, as heavy as the big metal doors to the gym at his old school.

As the doors swung slowly, Myron could see beyond a large room, lit blindingly through a skylight. Mignon Emanuel sat at an enormous desk, while Florence Agalega paced behind it, back and forth, back and forth.

"M-Miss Emanuel? Do—do you need anything else?" stammered Oliver.

"No, thank you, that will be quite sufficient."

"Maybe? M-maybe later I could . . ."

"Perhaps later, Oliver, thank you."

"Hello, Florence," Oliver squeezed in, and then he was gone, the doors shut tight behind him.

"Please have a seat," Mignon Emanuel said, rising briefly and gesturing at a small padded chair carved with many wooden swirls that stood before the desk, half resting on a tiger-skin rug. "Now," she smoothed her skirt into place as she sat back down, "we thought we could begin with your own account. If you would be so kind as to tell us what you know."

"What I know?" Myron hoped for further clarification, but Mignon Emanuel just nodded her head, so he continued. "I know that Oliver is not an immortal lycanthrope, but you guys are." He had not yet sat down. To reach the chair he would have to step on the tiger-skin rug, and he felt weird doing so. The head and jaws were still attached.

Mignon Emanuel asked, "Both of us?"

"Um. I don't know. I can feel that one's nearby, but I guess I don't know how many. You said you both were, though, before."

"Yes, your first assessment was correct, Myron. I merely wished to point out the danger of making assumptions. Modes of thought are one of the primary things we address here. What can you tell us about the state you refer to as immortal lycanthropy?"

Myron looked around the room. His eyes had adjusted to the bright sunlight, and he could see that the walls were covered with bookshelves, and the bookshelves were covered with books. In between some of the shelves were orna-mented panels with locks, which opened forward and down-ward, like an ironing board in the wall.

"The Unknown Men," he said, "said that we were origi-nally some kind of animal gods, for people to worship back in the days when people used to do that."

"That is certainly a very anthropocentric view of things," said Mignon Emanuel.

"A what now?" He had finally sat down.

"An anthropocentric view, a human-centered view. It as-sumes that we exist for the use of human beings. One might as well assume that human beings existed for our use."

"Did they? I mean, do they?"

Mignon Emanuel pushed her chair back and slid open a small drawer in the center of the desk. From it she took a small key, which she used to unlock one of the larger drawers. "There are many people here training their bod-ies, Myron, but it's important for you to train your mind. Humans tend to assume they're the most important crea-tures in the universe, and we can't let you fall into the same trap." She had meantime extracted from the drawer a large key ring filled with old-fashioned wrought-iron keys, the kind that looked like skeleton keys. Standing, she walked to the wall, unlocked a panel, and let it fall forward against her. From the nook she drew something rolled up and lami-nated. "What do you know about the revolution of the planets?"

The question surprised Myron. "The planets go around the sun, of course."

"Of course. But was this always the consensus of humanity?"

"No, people used to think the sun went around the earth."

"And they were wrong?"

"Sure, they were wrong."

"And how do you know this?" Mignon Emanuel was sitting down again, the laminated roll, its curl held by a rubber band, before her.

Myron fretted that Mignon Emanuel might be about to suggest something crazy. "Um. Science? I mean, if you sent a space probe up and looked down at the sun, it would see the earth rotating around it. Wouldn't it?"

"If the probe were to look down at the sun, yes; but what if it were to look down at the earth?"

"The probe stays where it is, and the earth would pass beneath it and travel on."

Emanuel nodded. "But how do you know the probe is standing still? You've assumed that it stands still if it stays above the sun, and you now assume that if it stands still the earth will move away from it. But you can't prove a conclusion if that conclusion has already been assumed in your premise. It's called *begging the question*. What if you assumed the earth stood still and the probe stood still looking down upon it?"

"Okay," Myron said, "forget the probe. The sun still doesn't move."

"Am I moving now?"

"No, you're sitting there. Oh, but you're going to say that you're moving because you're on the earth."

"And the earth is rotating on its axis, and revolving around the sun. But motion is relative. If you interpreted the question to mean *Am I moving in relation to the desk, or the room, or the ground,* then the answer is clearly *no.* I am not moving in relation to the earth. But if you interpreted it to mean *Am I moving in relation to the sun,* then the answer is *yes.* Do you understand? Then let me ask you, does the sun move?"

"What, in relation to other stars? Probably, but I don't know much about that."

"Well, the answer is yes, the sun moves in relation to other stars. Or you could say that other stars move in relation to the sun. On Earth we tend to agree, when we ask a question about motion, that we are referring to motion relative to the earth. But what do we mean when we refer to motion in space?"

"I don't know. Motion relative to the sun?"

"We could, of course, refer to motion relative to galactic clusters, but there's hardly a consensus on this point. Bringing other galaxies, or even other stars, into a model of the solar system makes as much sense as bringing the sun into a model of people moving around a room. We are free to choose a point and treat it as fixed, although this choice is arbitrary, as no point is truly fixed."

"Are you saying," Myron asked slowly, trying to wrap his head around the situation, "that the ancient astronomers were right?"

"No, of course not. Your hypothetical probe would prove Ptolemy wrong in an instant. I'm just saying that there is a workable model that places the earth at the center of the solar system." Here she slid the rubber band off the roll. It shot off the end, but Myron did not watch where it went; he was looking at what was on the laminated oak tag. It was a map of the solar system, of course. The map was peppered with numbers and annotations of apogees and perihelions that Myron could scarcely follow, but he could see the earth, labeled clearly in the center, with the moon orbiting it in a tight circle, the sun orbiting at some distance, with Mercury and Venus in concentric circles around the sun, Mars making a larger circle around everything, and then Jupiter, Saturn, and the rest, concentric around the orbit of Mars.

"This isn't a fair model," Myron snorted. "Look, it has Mercury and Venus go around the sun, not the earth."

"Every heliocentric model has the moon revolving around Earth, not the sun. These satellites are no different."

"But you're not saying that the sun goes around the earth, are you? Just that this version and the heliocentric version you mentioned are equally valid."

Mignon Emanuel tapped a glossy fingernail on the chart. "Let us be precise. An argument can be valid but still false, if one of its premises is untrue. I am saying that both this geocentric model and the heliocentric model are equally true."

Myron frowned over the strange symbols. "So should we use this one instead?"

"Probably not. Calculations are much more difficult to make with the model."

"What's this planet here at the edge? Proserpine? I've never heard of a planet called Proserpine."

"You've seen enough," said Mignon Emanuel, snapping the chart out from under Myron and rolling it up quickly. Florence silently handed over a rubber band, perhaps the same one that had gone flying, and then returned to pacing the room's perimeter. Mignon Emanuel replaced the roll in the cabinet and locked it again. The big ring of keys went into the big drawer, the small key into the small drawer. "Tell me," she went on, "what else you know about what you have referred to as *immortal lycanthropy.*"

Myron was worried for a moment that they would be there all day, if every question was followed by an astronomy lesson. Nevertheless, he marshaled his strength and pressed on: "They also said we were a dead branch, and there could be no new ones of us born."

"Another assumption of the Nine so-called Unknown Men, of whom no fewer than seven are currently known. Your existence is sufficient refutation and overthrow of the dead-branch model."

"And I know about the Time of Troubles, when everyone was murdering each other."

"It's possible to overstate the extent of the massacres, frankly."

"And I heard there is one of us for each animal species."

"Likely, if difficult to prove."

"But there are no marsupials."

"I can give evidence contradicting that hypothesis. I have met the swamp wallaby, *Wallabia bicolor,* an excellent fellow, as well as the wombat. Also most congenial, the wombat. *Vombatus ursinus.* There are monotremes, too."

"Monotremes?"

"Egg-laying mammals. *Monotreme* is Greek for *one-hole* in reference to their single exit to the excretory system."

"Oh. Like the platypus or the spiny echidna."

Mignon Emanuel rewarded Myron with a quick smile. "*Ornithorhyncus anatinus* is one of the deadliest opponents you're likely to face. He is the only venomous mammal—well, certain shrews and such may have a venomous bite, but they are too small to be of much notice. And he has a sixth sense, an ability to detect electricity, even the electric impulses in your nerves. A dastardly villain, *O. anatinus;* I was poisoned by him in a tragic incident, and have never quite recovered." She tugged at the collar of her blouse for a quick display of that nasty purple bruise. "I usually cover it with makeup. In human form it is unsightly, but I was poisoned as an animal, and I fear that—"

"Wait, what's poisonous?" Myron asked.

"*O. anatinus,* commonly called the duck-billed platypus."

"Platypi are poisonous?"

"Venomous. And don't say *platypi*—it is an incorrect

plural in Greek, Latin, and English. Platypodes or platypoda or even platypuses, if you must."

"I can't believe platypuses are venomous."

"I fear that if I turn back into *Procyon lotor* I will suffer a much worse fate."

"It works that way. Wounds from one form don't carry over?"

"No, of course not, but my human form is large enough that the venom is not fatal."

"As opposed to—what is your animal?"

"*P. lotor,* the raccoon. Small enough for the venom to kill. So I am stuck in human form until such a time as I can locate an antivenom capable of coping with immortal venom."

"And platypuses are seriously venomous?"

"They are."

"And what was that you said about their only having one hole?"

Mignon Emanuel explained this in more detail. What Myron took away from the lecture was that platypuses had sex with their butts, which is perhaps not strictly accurate.

"But we have spoken a long time, Myron, and you have much to think about. Permit me briefly to explicate the rules of this compound. In a word, there are no rules. You are in a land of do-as-you-please."

Myron remembered how nervous and respectful Oliver had been. "Oliver sure acted like he thought there were rules."

That earned another smile from Mignon Emanuel. She bestowed her smiles like gifts, or alms, and they were worth the wait. "For you there are no rules, to be more precise. Naturally not everyone has the same privileges as the chosen one."

Florence, who had been circling the room in her own unique orbit, added, "The boy's also an idiot. Factor that in."

"Now, do you have any questions for me?" Mignon Emanuel asked.

Myron was taken aback. But after a moment, without even a *yes,* he said, "I need to find out what happened to a friend of mine, this guy, Spenser."

"That was not a question."

"Can you help me?"

"Excellent. For I already am. I have met Spenser on several occasions, a splendid fellow, and when we found you we recognized his spoor. I have six woodsmen on his trail. The difficulty is that it appears he fled to Canada, and international red tape is retarding the proceedings."

"Can I go there? I don't mean Canada, I mean back to the place you found me."

"That will be difficult, for the location is three hundred miles away. I'm afraid you made quite a journey, much of it by boat, in your frozen state after we chanced across you. And with Marcus Lynch, *Panthera leo,* canonically nature's deadliest hunter, on your trail, I would hardly advise moving much past the front yard. I would not want you to worry, though, so I promise to keep you abreast of details. My only caveat is that the Spenser I knew was a consummate woodsman, and if he does not wish to be found, finding him will prove difficult."

"What do you know," Myron said, "about the bear?"

"There are too many species of bear to be certain of much. Also unknown is whether this was a strike, perhaps by *P. leo,* against you, or whether it was an unrelated event that only Spenser can shed light on."

"Okay, then let me ask about my parents."

"Your parents, happily, are safe. But I hope you understand that their safety is to some degree dependent on keeping a healthy distance from you."

"What? Why?"

"Myron, they are your weak spot. Any contact you have with them could, and probably will, be detected by your enemies."

"I don't believe this for one second," Myron shouted, standing up. "I've heard this story about my parents before!"

Mignon Emanuel pushed back her chair and stood as well. Myron hesitated, unsure whether she was standing because he had stood, to be polite, or whether she was going to start a fight. "I thought you might feel that way," she said, "so I encouraged an old friend of yours to join us." Clambering out from underneath the enormous desk came—

"Mrs. Wangenstein!" Myron cried. It was his old guidance counselor.

She said, nervously, "Myron, I'd like to take this opportunity to apologize for any inconvenience that might have been engendered from myself being compelled to be allied with your enemies. Full responsibility is of course taken by myself. I was blackmailed into it, it was not my fault. Photographs, a youthful indiscretion—"

"There's no need to go into the embarrassing details, my dear," Mignon Emanuel said. "We quite understand."

"Please be informed," Mrs. Wangenstein continued, "that while your family may have had their phone number reassigned to my husband and I's house, and I may have been compelled, through no fault of my own, to serve as an instrument, or rather a trusted lieutenant of your enemies, your family itself remains perfectly safe. This status of things was made certain of personally by myself. Their safety remains a priority of both Miss Emanuel and I, and it is my pleasure to inform you that they are residing in a series of luxury hotel accommodations. Their exact location remains uncertain even to someone as knowledgeable as myself.

"If wickeder people had not threatened, if the choice had not had to be made by myself between your enemies and Evelyn—"

"Thank you, Sophie," said Mignon Emanuel abruptly, her expression neutral. To Myron: "I hope this reassures you for the moment. If you would like to produce a letter, or a voice recording, we will make every effort, through our agents, to bring it to your parents' attention. Let us all work toward a time when such secrecy will no longer be necessary."

That seemed fairly final, if unsatisfying. "Okay," Myron said. "New question. Who's Evelyn?"

"*Loxodonta africana,* the African elephant. A terrible nuisance. There are more elements after you than you may know, Myron."

"Would you like myself to be returned back under the desk?" said Mrs. Wangenstein.

"No, please just stand," said Mignon Emanuel.

"Last question," Myron said. "Where am I?"

Later, when Myron left the room, he found Oliver hiding outside, waiting for him. No sooner did the heavy doors boom shut than he sidled up and in a harsh whisper asked, "What did Florence say about me?"

"I don't think she said anything at all," Myron said before he remembered that this was not true.

"I am so in love with her. Do you realize she's the only girl our age in a ten-mile radius?"

"I think she's older than I am."

"Miss Emanuel said you were thirteen. I'm almost fourteen, and Florence is probably fifteen. She may be too old for you, but I'm right in the zone." He wrapped his arms around himself and rocked back and forth. "Oh, Flossie! Flossie! Flossie!"

"Flossie?"

"And did you notice that she's shorter than me?"

"She's shorter than a lot of people."

"She's more beautiful than a lot of people. I'll pretend you meant that." He shook his fist menacingly.

"Miss Emanuel is very good-looking, too," Myron observed after some hesitation.

"She's completely unobtainable, and everyone is in love with her, even though she tells them she's five hundred years old. I should warn you, you should be less saucy around Miss Emanuel."

"Saucy?"

"I could hear a few things, accidentally, through the door. Not the words, just the tone of voice. And I've got to say, no one talks to her the way you do, not even Florence."

Myron hadn't meant to be particularly saucy. He was just tired of the runaround, tired of people he loved disappearing. He also rather liked Miss Emanuel, if tentatively, and he didn't find her intimidating. When he had been alone with her and Florence, he'd had the feeling that for the first time in a long time he was with people he could stand a chance against in a fight.

"Did you see the shape?"

"The what now?" Myron said. He had still been thinking, rather than paying attention to Oliver.

But now, "Come on," Oliver was saying, "I'll show you around."

Show him around where, though? Where was Myron? *Michigan* was the short answer, but Mignon Emanuel was fairly candid in her longer answer. The house in which he now stood had been built in the 1880s by bad architect Ricardo

Canuteson, and then rebuilt, with sounder structure but with the same rococo-gothic façade, in 1903. At more than one hundred thousand square feet, it had been, at one point, the largest private residence in Michigan. Rectangular in design, built around a central courtyard, with two flanking asymmetrical towers.

Myron didn't know what *rococo* meant, and scarcely knew what *gothic* meant in this context. Later, he would look them up, in the pocket dictionary on the bookshelf in his room, and not understand how they went together, until he made it outside and saw the place himself.

During the Depression, the building, and surrounding land, had been bought by the Knights of Pythias, a minor fraternal order best known for having in 1954 invented rock-and-roll music. They sold their acquisition in the seventies to a conglomerate of Qarmathian heretics from Bahrain. And *Panthera leo* fifteen years later picked it up from them with the money he had made in customized pornography. Originally the idea behind this gold mine was that pornographic stories, sold by subscription, could have a subscriber's name inserted as one of the characters; later, an innovation allowed combining two photos with an airbrush; the complexities of computer-aided photo or even film manipulation need hardly be belabored. Marcus Lynch did not invent customized pornography, but he ate the man who invented it, and thereby cornered the market.

But that was just money. Mignon Emanuel, who had

managed to wrest control of the house, had her own profits from various mail-order scams she only alluded to obliquely, as well as the sacks of cash found in the basement. But that was just money, too. Money was just step one. What was happening outside now, the muffled shouts and grunts, was step two: militia training.

Some forty years ago, Mignon Emanuel had (she explained) acquired a controlling share in a national chain of daycare centers, and during her tours of the individual franchises had carefully vetted each child for a particular combination of aggression and insecurity. Ten years later she had approached the selected children, one by one, in the afternoon as they left their high schools, invited them into a limousine and out to dinner—and implied she had known them in their youth, casually mentioned that she could offer them immortality, and left them with a photo. Ten years later another visit, another dinner. And then another. Sometimes, in the decades between, she would show up unexpectedly, with bail or a beer. Finally, in their midforties, the aging subjects were drawn by the increasingly plausible prospect of eternal youth and an offer few could resist to Michigan, where they spent their days and nights in tents outside this stately edifice, training along an obstacle course and in the arts of war. There were some desperate thirty-five-year-olds in there, too, from the second wave of daycare surveys. They came into the house only to do light housekeeping and cook meals—there was no staff proper. The only residents in the vast, empty building were Mignon Emanuel, Florence, Oliver, Mrs. Wangenstein (she nodded her head in proud acknowledgment of the mention), a certain Dr. Aluys, and, of course, young Myron Horowitz.

But the one hundred and thirty-three bruisers outside in their boxing rings and firing ranges, they were only step two. Step three was young Myron Horowitz.

Here Mrs. Wangenstein was sent from the room on some transparently false errand (counting orchids in the conservatory probably), and Mignon Emanuel leaned forward across the desk, not for the sake of secrecy, for she spoke in a normal voice, but as one leans toward a friend, a friend about to receive monumental and joyous news. "I'm engaged!" "I'm having a baby!" "I got the job!" That kind of news.

She said, "Imagine an army of us, an immortal army capable of infiltrating any camp, of flying, burrowing, or brachiating"—she actually used this word, I have it on good authority—"and incapable of being stopped." Myron looked a little worried, and Mignon Emanuel changed her tone. "Imagine, as well: We are the only one who can kill us. Why do we keep doing it? Why can we not live peacefully with each other? Humanity has offered us the trappings of civilization, and we have chosen, repeatedly chosen, to live by the law of tooth and claw. Do you see the common problem here?"

Myron did not.

"We live in anarchy. We have no organizing principles;

we acknowledge no government or sovereignty. In the reign of chaos, all there can be is violence; the violence of the cat against the mouse, of the strong against the weak. There has never been anyone to raise a voice in an attempt to persuade our brethren toward unity. Until now."

"Me?" said Myron.

"You're the proof that we are not a dead branch, Myron. You're the hope that there may, indeed, be more to come." Mignon Emanuel had stood up now, and walked around the huge desk to kneel by Myron's chair. When Florence came to stand next to her, they were the same height. "You offer us, you offer them something to live for, Myron. They'll never forget you for that. But there are a few—Marcus is one, Evelyn, yes, is another—who seek leadership for their own nefarious ends. You are in danger from them, true, but here, surrounded by these elite guards, you'll be safe until your enemies can be converted to your point of view."

Myron was excited. "So what do we do?"

"Leave that to me, Myron. I've already set the wheels in motion, the great wheels, you might say, on which revolve the heavens." Her smile at this point was jaw busting and absolutely delightful. "Your grand debut is already scheduled, when your unique status will be revealed, first to the human members of the Invisible College"—here she meant the various secret societies Myron had met and would meet—"and later to the rest of us, whom you are destined to rule, with

Florence and me at your side to advise, of course. It will be an exciting time, Myron, and there's every chance, as word gets around, that our friend Spenser will hear about it and learn you're safe. But while we prepare for the occasion, please, look around, let Oliver show you the ropes, have a good time, and relax."

Myron would hardly believe his good fortune. "Is Oliver," he asked, after a moment, "one of the daycare center recruits? Because he's awful young."

"No, Oliver is a different matter altogether. Show it to him, Florence."

Florence drew over her head a leather thong that had been resting outside her turtleneck. Coming up along with it, from behind the front bib of her purple overalls, was a molded piece of gray plastic. It was flat, and its outline was curved.

"What's that?" Myron asked, as Florence held the thong; the plastic piece twisted back and forth.

"That," Florence said, "is the shape."

3.

Oliver showed Myron all the best places to hide, the coal chute, the drop ceiling, showed him the secret passage from behind the orchids to the lounge, and the one banister you probably should not slide on. "I know every inch of this building, I know mysterious places no one else has ever been, probably," Oliver explained. In one bathroom the tub had feet. Myron was still woozy, so they spent a great portion of the day watching the troops go through their paces on the obstacle course. They were middle-aged, so it was not so easy to whip them into fighting shape, but they were trying. At night, in the kitchen, Oliver boiled water in an electric kettle and brought down packets of instant oatmeal.

"You may not want to watch this," Oliver said. "I like my oatmeal really thick, and it grosses some people out. I mean really, really thick."

Myron peeked over at what he was stirring in the bowl. "That's not too bad," he said, "that's only a little bit thicker than I would make it." Then Oliver dumped another packet of oatmeal into the mix. So that happened.

Then they rode back and forth on the rolling ladders in the library. Myron found a handsome set of uniform editions of the complete works of H. Rider Haggard and another of the complete works of Jules Verne, and he took a couple of volumes up to his tower, where he read, at last, until he fell asleep. Every day went more or less like that. Oliver was always around, and, when he slunk off on his own business, Myron returned to his tower room. Outside were a hundred and thirty-three men, but in the long days in the big house they seemed miles away. Sometimes when Myron and Oliver went to the kitchen to swipe cold cuts, one of the men would be there, too, fixing food, and he would explain things about anatomy that Myron could not follow.

On many evenings, Mignon Emanuel would assign Oliver some menial and arduous task and then call Myron into her office and, while Florence paced ceaselessly behind them, give him lessons in the hidden patterns that underlay, as she called it, the "phenomenal world." They covered the golden ratio and the Fibonacci sequence; the dangers of confirmation bias; Zipf's law; and some basic predicate logic. These evenings Myron would take a problem set to the tower, to finish before the next lesson. In some ways, this labor could be boring and frustrating, but it was also exciting. He was learning forbidden lore. He also didn't want to disappoint Mignon Emanuel, for reasons he would have been hard-pressed to explain. But the lessons caused some awkwardness, too, for Oliver resented them, and Mrs. Wangenstein, for reasons of her own, expressed on several occasions her disapproval of learning outside a "sanctioned school environment."

A couple of times a week there would be a big dinner, prepared by the recruits, and the five housemates would sit at the huge dining-room table. An extra place was always set, but it was always empty. Mignon Emanuel would carve the duck, or the lamb, offer around a side of salmon, and propose toast after toast until Mrs. Wangenstein slid out of her chair, weeping and apologizing to everyone and her absent family. Myron tasted a little of the wine, and learned that the sip he took was worth almost two hundred dollars. Oliver drank three glasses, and began to vomit, which got the sobbing Mrs. Wangenstein vomiting, too. This happened more than once. At first Myron thought the sip of wine made him feel so strange, but eventually he realized it was the salmon. Several weeks went by.

One day alarms sounded, the militiamen mobilized outside, and a car ground along the gravel drive. Mignon Emanuel and Florence came to the door to meet it, which was unusual, and Myron and Oliver hung around to see what would happen. Out of the car stepped—Benson! He wore a leather duster and mirror shades, and over his shoulder he balanced a shotgun. Myron began to panic, but Benson just wanted to talk to Mignon Emanuel. Their rather strained and trite conversation went something like:

"You know Lynch knows you have him," from Benson.

"It was bound to happen."

"Don't be stupid, just hand him over. Lynch has a lot of contacts."

"Tell him you've seen that I have contacts here, too. He's welcome to come, you know, even if I didn't get around to sending an invitation."

"He knows about the conference next week. He must know about the little trick you can do by now, too."

"Truth be told, I've been having a little trouble with that. It's why I had to leave. But the boy's safe here, tell him that. Oh, and, Benson"—melodramatically, over her shoulder, as she turned away. "I could always use more muscle."

"Yeah, well. I could always use a good driver." They nodded to each other, and Benson left. Myron's heart returned to its usual location.

The next day another car with visitors came, which the murmuring of the mobilized grunts indicated was very unusual.

Oliver and Myron came running again, but they missed the introductions. Once again, Mignon Emanuel was standing in the doorway, the guests on the porch. Florence paced back and forth nervously.

"They're all Indian," whispered Oliver, hidden down the hall behind a late Roman reproduction of a Greek statue of Dionysus.

"And they're not wearing hats," Myron noted. "*Very* interesting."

"You're a little early," Mignon Emanuel was saying.

One of the three Indians adjusted his tie awkwardly. "We actually aren't going to be able to come to the conference. We just thought it needful to warn you—"

"Threats aren't warnings," Mignon Emanuel said. She had clearly lost all interest in the conversation.

"This is not a threat; make no mistake. It's one of our own, Dantaghata, a very junior member, we fear he may be coming this way. This has none of our sanction—"

"Don't play innocent. If he's of such low rank, how would he even know to come here?"

"He's been talking to Meridiana. You know no one can control what Meridiana tells one."

"Meridiana," Myron whispered to Oliver, "is their brazen head."

"Know-it-all," said Oliver.

Mignon Emanuel was looking off into the distance. "Yes, yes. Well, I can take care of myself. Now, if you'll excuse—"

"Kindly listen, he even managed to steal from us the astra. The astra of the gods."

"Take better care of your things. Good day." And she slammed the door. Through a window, Myron watched the militia jeer and catcall as the three Unknown Men drove away. It was the most excitement they'd seen since Myron had shown up.

Later that day, Myron and Oliver were walking idly down one of the labyrinthine corridors. Myron was trying to gauge how much Oliver knew about his upcoming debut—the answer appeared to be *nothing*—when Myron felt something familiar and awful. His legs buckled, and he fell over. He thought he was going to die, so when Oliver nudged him with his toe, Myron said, "I just slipped."

"I wouldn't lie on the carpet, man. The soldiers are kind of halfhearted housecleaners."

Myron struggled to his feet, and, his head still swimming, looked around. The impulse came from a door, a door like any other in the house. Myron staggered over to it and tried the handle, but of course it was locked. From the large keyhole came a kind of miasma.

"Can you smell that? I mean, can you feel that?" Myron said.

"Are you on drugs?"

The keyhole was keyhole-shaped, of course, but Myron had never seen, before coming to this house, a keyhole in that shape. With infinite care, he put his eye up to it, but the far side of the door was dark.

"That door's always locked. Come on—let's go."

"Well, what's on the other side?"

"I don't know, I tried picking the lock with a mechanical pencil last night when you were whacking off, but it didn't work. No one knows what's past locked doors, and no one cares."

"I have to go see Miss Emanuel," Myron said.

"Are you crazy? You can't just go and see her, you wait for her to summon you." This was said with some bitterness, as Oliver was, frankly, rarely summoned.

"No, it'll be fine, come with me."

"You're literally nuts, I'm not getting in trouble for that." And after some more of this classic back-and-forth, Oliver left, and Myron staggered back to the office, the office with the double doors and the brass plaque. He had realized he didn't know where else to look for her.

The farther he went, the more his head cleared until, standing again in front of the double doors, he found himself knocking, and then ringing the buzzer. No one answered, and Myron turned to go.

Suddenly he felt his neck prickle. Florence was coming down the corridor. "Come with me," she said, and, removing a key from the snowflake pocket of her romper, on tiptoes opened the office door.

There sat Mignon Emanuel at the big desk. Myron was surprised to see that the office was, in fact, occupied, and he looked around for a door she might have come through.

"The bookshelf is on hinges," Mignon Emanuel said, guessing his confusion, "and it is through this that I entered. Now, what can I help you with?"

"I found a locked door."

"There are many locked doors. Behind the bookshelf is a locked door. I keep it locked because my bedroom suite is on the far side, and I do value my privacy. I believe Florence often locks her bedroom door as well."

Florence nodded.

"You said there were no rules here," Myron protested.

"Locking a door is hardly a rule. If I were to forbid you to try to pick the lock, that would be a rule, but not granting you access through a locked door is no more a rule than not letting you fly. It's not my rule; it's gravity's."

Myron wasn't sure that made sense, but he let it slide. "I was curious what's behind the door. It's the one down the corridor on the kitchen side of the grand ballroom. Past the red room?"

They knew which door he was talking about. Suddenly the tenor of the conversation changed. Florence took a half step away from Myron. Mignon Emanuel's eyes became cagey.

"Why are you curious about that room?" she asked.

Already Myron was saying, "It reminded me of—" And his guard was down enough that he was ready to talk about the doomsday device, and the way it had made him feel in Greenwich Village. But everyone was being so extraordinarily cautious that he instinctively stopped.

Of? Mignon Emanuel did not say. But her eyes said it.

In Myron's head swam, whenever he was called upon to lie, his memories of heroes and their deceptions, of Huck Finn dressed as a girl, of David Balfour dressed as a Jacobite, of Sherlock Holmes or Raffles—masters of disguise, of Long John Silver, pathologically. This was how he thought, and how he lied, and he rather wished he could stop lying quite so much. But when he looked in Mignon Emanuel's face, he found himself saying, "—of something Spenser once mentioned. About a door he'd seen, once, long ago."

There was one of those awkward moments, then, when it became clear that Mignon Emanuel wanted Myron to leave, and Myron wanted to leave, but neither one could admit it, and so they stood. Mignon Emanuel made eye contact with Florence, and Florence, Myron noticed, raised her eyebrows inquiringly, but Mignon, after a moment's hesitation, shook her head, a tiny, quick shake. It was probably meant to be imperceptible, but Mignon Emanuel never moved quickly, so it stood out by contrast. Finally, after a few false pleasantries, Myron all smiles stepped out of the room. And as soon as the door was shut, he ran. He ran down the long corridor to the study, practically slid through the secret passage, and in ten more steps he was at the base of the tower, at the base of the endless staircase. Up which he ran. His legs were perhaps still wobbly, but he had been recovering quickly; his winter in the woods had hardened him somewhat, and an upstairs run he never could have made six months ago he managed with only a stitch in his side and the rising bile of nausea as he half fell up the last step into his room. There squatted Oliver, frozen in midrummage. He had been rummaging through the duffle bag.

His mouth, when he saw Myron, opened and closed lamely. Finally, "I lost my protractor," he said. "Do you think maybe I left it in here?"

"Get out," Myron said.

"I'm not fibbing," Oliver said, but he left. Myron kicked the door shut, dived under the bed, and came up with—the cardboard tube was there, the doomsday device was safe. Wrapping it in a bathrobe for camouflage, he ran back down the endless staircase, his eyes cast back and forth for a sign of Oliver, or any others, and zigged down one hall, zagged up another, carefully to deposit the tube inside the vast maw of what was probably not but may have been an actual Ming vase.

Then, worrying he might have left something else behind, he turned and ran back, back to the staircase that loomed again in its infinite spiral. He was gasping like a drowning man by the time he reached the top of the tower, and as he stepped up to the threshold his neck prickled, and he saw something scurrying in the bull's-eye window. It looked like a monkey, with a cat's face marked distinctively in black and white like a radiation symbol. Its long monkey tail was zebra striped, and it was holding a large piece of red silk. There was something around its neck. Myron was breathing too hard to say anything, but he had the presence of mind to drop the bathrobe he was still carrying, stealthily on the step behind him, just out of sight from the room. His first thought, truth be told, was that it was a raccoon horribly deformed by platypus venom. His second thought was that *P. leo,* king of beasts, had strange beasts at his command. But his third thought was correct. And the creature leapt down, behind the bed, and came up in a swirl of red. It was Florence, belting a loose kimono around her.

"Emanuel was worried about you, you left in such a hurry," she said.

"It took you that long to get up here, and you're a monkey?"

"A lemur. And I got up here fast enough, but—well, you might as well know, the kid was in here, going through your things."

"And you couldn't come in, because he doesn't know."

"He doesn't know unless you told him. I thought you would, Emanuel thought you wouldn't." She shrugged. "So I went looking for you. Frankly, I thought you would have gotten here faster, I took so long trying to find you before I returned."

Myron realized that she didn't know, somehow she

didn't know he'd been there and back. Maybe she'd gone all the way back to consult with Mignon Emanuel about what Oliver was doing. Or maybe, Myron thought for a moment, maybe she was telling the truth, and nothing but simple concern had brought her up here.

But then, "Do you think Oliver might have taken anything? Maybe we should take stock of all your things," Florence suggested, and Myron knew that something strange was going on.

"By all means," said Myron, trying not to sound canny. "Just let me catch my breath." And together they went through the duffle bag, Myron's clothes, his toothbrush, his polished soda can, the borrowed Verne and Haggard volumes, the compound bow . . .

"Are you missing anything? Is this all?"

"I had a cardboard tube with some waterlogged comic books and pinups and things in it, but it had gotten all wet in the snow, so I threw it out days ago." Myron had resolved to play it close to the vest.

Florence took a quick peep under the bed.

"So what are you again? A lemur?" Myron said. He vaguely remembered learning about lemurs in school.

"Ring-tailed lemur. From Madagascar."

"From Madagascar?" Myron awkwardly tried to remember if pygmies lived in Madagascar. He wished suddenly he'd been paying more attention in social studies class.

But Florence explained briefly that she was not of the

same people as the current inhabitants of Madagascar. Her people, the Vazimba, had flourished in Madagascar for thousands of years before the outriggers came from the east. They brought death to her people, who were very short, and not very good at fighting the long war clubs. Florence stole an outrigger canoe and set off to the east with a handful of Vazimba to find the homeland of the invaders, but only made it to the Agalega Islands where, over the agonizing years, one by one, everyone died but her. After some centuries she returned, on a piece of driftwood to Madagascar, and found that all the Vazimba were gone with scarcely a trace, except in legend.

The story was too sad for Myron to know how to respond. He was used to the despair of Spenser's stories, of course, but that was all philosophical despair. It was hardly personal, it was just the way of the world. Florence told the story in a flat and unaffected tone, but it was so clearly personal nonetheless.

"Did you ever go back to the Agalega Islands?" Myron asked.

"Oh yeah. I was a pirate queen there a hundred and fifty years ago. That was a good time to be a pirate."

"Maybe," Myron suggested tentatively, "maybe you have a story about pirates, too?"

And she did! They had a grand old time there, talking pirate talk, which Myron had picked up from Robert Louis Stevenson and R. M. Ballantyne and Jack London. After a while, when they were both feeling a little giddy, Myron asked if he could see the shape. Florence removed it from around her neck and handed it to him. It was heavier than he had thought.

"I don't get this," Myron said.

"You're not supposed to get it."

"Why do you have to be the one who has to carry it?"

"It makes sense. I can get away easily if Oliver decided to really go after it."

"That's what I don't get. Why would he want to?"

"He doesn't have a choice. He's another experiment from another daycare center; an experiment to get children addicted to various objects, and in that way make them utterly loyal to whoever could provide them. I don't know all the details, or if they put electrodes in his brain or what, but he ended up addicted to a certain shape: that one. It's a hard shape to copy, although sometimes you'll see him try to cut it out of cardboard."

He handed it back. "There are others like him, then?"

"No, I think all the others went insane."

"Insane?"

"Or died, or something, I don't really know. He's the only one it worked on." And since Florence was, for the reason stated above, usually the one to carry the shape around, this explained, she said, Oliver's unnatural (unnatural because lemurs and humans should not mix) attraction to her.

"This all sounds horrible."

"I'm sure it's not as bad as I'm making it sound. Most of this happened when I was still operating in Guatemala. I didn't hook up with Emanuel till later."

"Is it just coincidence, then, that you and Miss Emanuel are both ringtails?"

"Ringtail? What tail are you talking about there?"

"Her raccoon tail, of course. Raccoons have ringed tails, don't they?"

"Oh! Oh, I was thinking of something else. Yes, of course she has a ringtail too, but that's just a coincidence. And speaking of Emanuel, I'd better go tell her you're doing swell." And at that, the lemur was back, sitting in the voluminous folds of the red kimono. She wadded the silk up in one tiny hand and leapt to the window, and then scrabbled down the brown, dead ivy along the tower. She had clearly been lying about something.

Myron lay down on his bed and stared at the ceiling and wondered whom to trust.

VII

The Conference in the Fortress of the Id

This is a great and terrible world. I never knew there were so many men alive in it.

Rudyard Kipling, *Kim*

I.

It is an open question, how much impact one has on one's own fate. Reasonable philosophers seem to argue for *some*. Certainly Myron Horowitz may often appear as a pawn, buffeted will-I nill-I by the hand of an unseen player, or by a cat that leaps on the board. But his was a restless soul, happy only on the move, that could never be satisfied with life at the top of Rapunzel's tower, however pleasant the palace itself. So I ask you: to what extent did he orchestrate his own expulsion from paradise, or, if not paradise, from a warm bed, fine food, and a tastefully selected library? The chain of events that climaxed in him fleeing alone into the dark forests at night—did he wind it around himself?

I was relaxing over a cup of tea in my Boston brownstone. Alice would not get off the phone, demanding to know what I had learned so far. Somewhere in the inaudible distance a lion must have been roaring ominously, plotting how to get to his prey. At the fortress, in the backyard, the snow was melting away, with odd piles lingering around the fringes, by the woods. It was still cold out, but Myron had a new winter coat and a long, soft scarf; when the militiamen were at mess, he and Oliver would play around on the obstacle course. There were guards posted, and the guards had guns, and harpoon guns, inexplicably, too, but they turned a blind eye as Myron and Oliver swung on ropes and climbed on tires and failed to scale the wall they were too short to jump up to.

One morning the obstacle course was unexpectedly empty, and the boys had it to themselves for a long time. They had brought Myron's compound bow out and were practicing firing sticks from it, as they had no arrows. After a while, Florence came out and joined them. She was, as always, a battery of nervous energy, and climbed up and down some knotted ropes to show the world how it was done.

"That's what we need," said Oliver. "We need special training. Flossie, you should be making us punch bags of rice or stand under a waterfall."

Florence waved the suggestion away, and climbed up and down some more things, but Oliver pressed. He wanted to have a contest between him and Myron, and he wanted Florence to judge. Whoever won the contest would get a prize. "We could run the obstacle course, and then we could have a race, and then we could get in the boxing ring."

"I really don't want to do this," Myron said.

Florence was sitting on top of the tall wooden crosspiece from which the ropes depended. She was looking down, but it was not clear that she was listening.

Oliver picked a pair of boxing gloves off the ground, where they'd been dropped, and tossed them over to Myron. "Come on, put these on."

Myron refused. Oliver had in the meantime slid gloves on his own fists. He couldn't lace them up, of course, and they were far too large for him. They flopped back and forth loosely on his wrists.

"Put up your dukes, Myron!" Oliver cried. He began to dance around Myron, bobbing and weaving.

"This is not a legal match," Myron said. "We're not even in the ring."

"Ding," said Oliver, and he went in. He started tentatively, with a little light bodywork, his jabs barely touching Myron, who was endeavoring to squirm out of the way; but as he went on, and noticed that Florence was hardly even looking at him, he began to punch more in earnest.

"Quit it," Myron said, his bare hands up shielding his face.

"The champ is on the ropes," Oliver said. "How long can he stand up to this punishment?" The blows that landed were hardly solid, the gloves too limp and floppy to allow much force, but they stung nevertheless.

"Looks like the new kid from Vancouver is ready to claim the belt."

"Stop it, I mean it."

"The crowd is going wild!"

Myron felt tears welling up in his eyes. He'd been hurt much worse than this before, of course, but there was something galling about the way this would not stop. It just kept going and would not stop. Stepping backwards, he tripped on the gloves he'd refused to put on and fell over. In a moment, Oliver was on top of him, his legs pinning Myron's arms. He was pounding ineffectually, with the underside of the glove, like a masseur, but he was pounding directly on Myron's face. Myron began to scream.

"Florence!" A loud voice carried clearly from up above, and Oliver stopped. He turned his head. From a second-story window Mignon Emanuel was leaning. "Florence, could you bring Myron to my office?"

Suddenly noticing what was going on, Florence scampered down the rope. She pulled Myron to his feet. Oliver was standing nearby, his face downcast.

Mignon Emanuel called down, "And Oliver. That's three days without, and five hours KP. Do you understand?"

Oliver stomped his foot and let out a long glottal-fricative sigh.

From the window: "I said, do you understand?"

"Yes, ma'am," said Oliver at a volume perfectly pitched just barely to reach the second floor.

Florence took Myron to a washroom, cleaned his face up a bit, gently, and then brought him to the office.

"What were you thinking?" was the first thing Mignon Emanuel said as they entered.

"I'm not very good at boxing," Myron said.

Mignon Emanuel ignored him. "What if he had panicked and changed, in front of the guards and everyone?"

"I wasn't paying attention," Florence said.

"We're three days away from the conference, and your not paying attention could ruin everything."

Florence glared right back. "I've already said I'm sorry," she said, which Myron noted wasn't strictly true. "It won't happen again. What more do you want from me?"

Mignon Emanuel did not look happy, but she turned her attention to Myron. "You've had a scare," she said. "Would you like to go lie down, or would you be able to help me with something?"

"I could help," said Myron.

And so Florence took Myron to Mrs. Wangenstein's room, and Mrs. Wangenstein measured him with a tape measure. She wrote all the numbers down on a little pad with a golf pencil she liked to lick.

"Was that all?" Myron asked as Mrs. Wangenstein scurried off with the pad.

"That was all."

"What's going to happen to Oliver?" Myron asked. He didn't really like Oliver, but he couldn't get over the thought of the experiment he had gone through. Also, where the heck were his parents?

"He'll be peeling potatoes for a while." And Myron was left alone. Everyone was busy, and he had nothing to do. He sat on his bed and groused, because all of this was supposed to be for him.

In the evening, Myron was called, as he often was, from his room to dinner by a complicated code of bells. Mignon Emanuel and Florence were already there when he arrived, and he was about to ask them about the conference, about what his role, his leadership role, would be in the new world they were working toward. But before he could, a very old man in a doorman's coat with lace coming out the sleeves entered.

"Who?" said Myron.

"*Bonjour,*" said the old man. "I am Dr. Aluys." He swept his arm around in a great arc and bowed. And Mrs. Wangenstein came scurrying in. The main course was pheasant, with a side of salmon, and as usual no one talked.

Myron tried to catch Mignon Emanuel's attention with his eyes, to ask about Dr. Aluys, but she was looking resolutely at her plate, or into the distance. He caught Florence's eye and raised an inquiring eyebrow, as he'd seen her do once, but just then Oliver came in and, perceiving everything instantly, sat down and kicked Myron repeatedly under the table until Myron drew his feet up and sat on his knees. He then kicked Myron several times in the knees, but this was more difficult for him to do, so at last he stopped. Nevertheless, Myron was getting annoyed.

Perhaps it was for this reason that when Oliver asked if

he could pour himself some wine, and Mignon Emanuel assented, Myron waited until he was halfway through the task before uttering, loudly, the ancient words he had learned from Spenser: "Pax sax sarax . . ."

Oliver dropped the bottle, which shattered on the white tablecloth. Red wine shot out sideways, leaving a splatter pattern like a beheading's. Mrs. Wangenstein, for her part, began to vomit everywhere, which was curious as she had had nothing to drink yet. Oliver half fell out of his chair before he caught himself. Whatever Myron expected to happen, this was something quite extraordinary. Mignon Emanuel's eyes narrowed.

"Perhaps you had better not repeat that," she said, for it had been a 1990 La Tâche Burgundy.

And from the far side of the table, the old man, Dr. Aluys, began to laugh and laugh.

Mrs. Wangenstein went back to her room. By dessert, Oliver was making light of the incident. Primeval words of power did not impress him, he insisted. "It's a simple parlor trick; that's all. Like when psychics bend spoons with their mind. Big deal! If I concentrated that hard, I could do it, too! It's just not worth it." Oliver then proceeded to demonstrate how easily he could bend spoons using brute strength and the principle of leverage. He'd done two before Mignon Emanuel reminded him that he was in enough trouble already. At that he jumped out of his chair so fast that the chair tipped over, and on the way out he bumped Myron with his shoulder.

Mignon Emanuel still bore an accusatory look, when she looked at Myron. "You said there were no rules!" Myron said.

"This is the land of do-as-you-please, and there are no rules. But even in the land of do-as-you-please there are repercussions for your actions. I do not dictate, but I suggest, that you avoid trotting out whatever ancient lore you have acquired. At the very least, it makes dinner more awkward, and robs us of the pleasure of a fine Burgundy. Furthermore, it might make people doubt you are as young as you are."

"I learned it from Spenser, I'd never heard anything like it before that."

"Doubtless. Florence and I have spoken such tongues at certain points in our lives—dark, twisted tongues from forgotten times, as well. But your proficiency in one, I hope you understand, could engender suspicion. Again, I am merely here to suggest ramifications. The responsibility of decision is your own."

Myron felt embarrassed by what he'd done, and the reasonableness with which Mignon Emanuel was accepting it only made it worse. But he was tired of living a life of constant suspicion. The terrible adventure had begun to wear him down. He wanted to trust Mignon Emanuel, he wanted to believe that he could relax his guard. But his guard was still up, and his nerves were frayed.

"What about him?" Myron said, pointing at Dr. Aluys.

"He's just a guy, isn't he, a human? How come he's not affected by the forgotten speech?"

"One's humanity has nothing to do with this," Mignon Emanuel said. "It's merely a question of getting used to it."

Myron looked over at the old man. How did he get used to it?

With a pleasant nod, he answered: "*Mon chéri,* I have seen so many things your young eyes would not believe. If your eyes, they are truly young."

"Hmm," said Myron.

Mignon Emanuel went on, "I know it's been difficult for you, Myron, but in three days we have the conference, and we'll need to be at our best."

"That's what I don't even know anything about! What's the deal with the conference?"

"Haven't you been paying attention, Myron? Please, it's very important that you pay attention. You should already know all about the conference, and I'm not about to review matters you should have mastered long ago. You'll be presented at last as the chosen one, the first to be born in millennia."

"But what will I do? You said there'd be people coming. Why won't there be any immortal lycanthropes?"

"It's nigh impossible to get any of us to do anything organized. That's why we're starting with other people, people with contacts, who can get the word out and generate interest."

"I'm supposed to be in charge, don't I get to decide who to invite? The Nine Unknown Men won't even be there!"

"The Nine Unknown Men have sent their regrets, and the Rosicrucians are too scared to stir from their West Coast sanctuary. But there will be a great many influential people in attendance. If you don't mind saying a few words, I'll gladly take the liberty of having some apposite remarks typed up."

If Myron had been thinking straight, he would have been terrified by the idea, but he was angry, and distracted by the mention of the Rosicrucians. "Who are they? Why does everyone talk about them?" he demanded.

"Hardly anyone perspicacious ever talks about them anymore," said Mignon Emanuel, ending the discussion.

After dinner he walked past the room again, the room that had made him dizzy, and there was nothing there, no feeling. The door was still locked. He went up to his tower in a great funk, and Oliver was there and hit him across the head with a two by four.

2.

Myron awoke strapped spread-eagled on a table. His head ached, and his tongue felt furry. His first thought was that he has been knocked unconscious entirely too many times recently. His second thought was pure panic. He was in a laboratory. Along a bench by the wall was strange glassware, test tubes and alembics and spiral tubing, all covered in cobwebs.

He didn't know what most of the devices were, but he didn't like them much. Over to one side, where he could barely see, was a kind of crib or cage with something moving in it.

"Hello?" Myron tried to say, but found he had been gagged.

Darting into his angle of vision suddenly was Oliver, wearing an overlarge lab coat and holding a beaker filled with liquid. A glass straw stuck out of the beaker.

"You're going to tell me where it is," Oliver said.

"I can't tell you anything with this gag in my mouth," Myron failed to enunciate.

Oliver held the glass straw and put his thumb over its top. When he lifted the straw up, the liquid inside stayed there.

"This is acid," Oliver said. "Or it's probably acid—I can't read most of this stuff. What is this, is this Spanish? What's an *'extrêmement dangereux'*?" He held the straw over Myron's arm and lifted his thumb up. The liquid slipped out, and when it hit his sleeve, it began to . . . to sizzle is perhaps the right word. In a moment it had worked its way through the shirt and burned his skin. Myron was so surprised by the pain that he shouted with sufficient vigor to expel the gag from his mouth. The gag, it turned out, was nothing more than an old pair of underpants that had been wadded in there.

"Go ahead and scream," Oliver said. "No one ever comes down here. No one even knows this place exists."

Myron writhed in frustration. "What about the thing in the cage over there?" he said, trying to keep Oliver's attention away from the acid.

"He's not going to talk."

"I mean, someone comes to feed him, clearly."

"He's half dead of starvation."

"Look, Oliver, you have to listen to me. This isn't even going to work, you can't kill me."

"Excuse me, are you the Virgin Mary? Because you are *making an assumption!* You are assuming I want to kill you."

"I don't understand what that means, I'm Jewish!"

Silently, Oliver put the acid away and picked up a hacksaw.

Myron tried, "Oliver, you're going to get in trouble for this."

"You won't know anything about that, you'll be dead."

"I knew it!" He shook his bindings in frustration. "Oliver, I'm immortal. Miss Emanuel is as well, and Florence. We can all turn into animals!"

"Miss Emanuel warned me that you were delusional and might try telling me something like this." He laid the saw across Myron's abdomen.

"Oliver, please think clearly. Are you trying to kill me, or are you trying to extract information from me?"

Oliver had gotten a little ahead of himself, and after a moment's reflection he had to admit, "First one and then the other."

"I know where Mignon Emanuel keeps a second shape. I've been working on the puzzle all this time."

"Aha!" Oliver jumped in the air with glee. "I knew there was a second shape, I knew you'd crack."

"It's in the locked room, the one we saw the day you— the day you lost your protractor."

"That's right, I did lose my protractor. But if it's in the locked room, we'll never get it."

"I know where Mignon Emanuel keeps the keys. They're in the desk in her office. All we need to do is get into her office."

"We'll never do that."

In the crib in the corner, something unseen scuttled about.

Myron said, "I have a plan. We can do this together, Oliver, but I need you to do it. You know about this conference, right? I'm going to have to make a speech, and right before I go on, I'm going to say I lost the speech, the paper with the speech on it. And you'll be around, and you'll say you'd found it but slipped it under the door to the office because you thought it was hers. And we'll need the speech so she'll have to send one of us to go get it. Do you see, Oliver? We can get the key!"

"She'll send Florence, not us."

"We'll have to get rid of Florence somehow." For a moment, Myron saw wrath blaze in Oliver's eyes, and he quickly amended his statement. "We'll send her on a fool's errand,

I mean. We have three days to think of a plan. But it won't work without both of us. What do you say, Oliver?"

Oliver was shaking. But his shaking head nodded. He began to unknot the strap binding Myron's wrist, which proved to be the tie from a bathrobe threaded through a handy staple in the table. As he struggled with it, a voice called out.

"Oliver!" It was Mignon Emanuel. She was standing on the rickety stairs leading down to the room. Florence was with her, and was already sprinting down the staircase, ducking under the banister when halfway down to jump five feet to the floor.

"We were playing!" Oliver cried.

"It's true, we're just playing," Myron said, "but I'm getting a little bored. Can you untie me?"

In a moment, Florence had undone the three knots and the belt buckle, and Myron was free. He could see that Mignon Emanuel was already turning away, back up the stairs. The crib in the corner looked like it held an alligator.

"There's blood on the floor of your room," Florence whispered. "Emanuel got worried."

"That's from a nosebleed, from before. We're just goofing around, but I think Oliver began to lose it at one point. Seriously, he needs the shape."

"He's off it for three days."

"Seriously. He needs the shape." Myron tried to make it clear with his face how important it was.

How much Oliver, who'd spent the time paralyzed with terror, heard of this is debatable. But when Florence took the shape out from the neck of her jumper, Oliver scurried over and fell to his knees. She put one arm around him as he stroked the shape and wept. Silently, Myron turned and slunk away. He crept up the stairs.

From this angle it became clear that the alligator had the rear legs, rump, and tail of a donkey.

No time to think about that! Myron hit the top of the stairs and began to run. He didn't have much of a plan, but he thought maybe if he beat Mignon Emanuel to her office he could hide in some way that would let him slip in after her. She could go through her secret bookcase passage, and he'd be at liberty to plunder the desk for a key. He took every shortcut Oliver had taught him, but when he rounded the final corner, Mignon Emanuel was already stepping through her office door. She suddenly turned around to look over her shoulder, but Myron ducked back around the corner before he could be noticed, and ran away. And then he caught his breath. He realized that the back of his neck had not prickled at all.

This explained why he had never seen Mignon Emanuel without Florence there as well. Perhaps with more experience he would have been able to distinguish between the presence of one and two immortal lycanthropes, but he was still new at this, and had never noticed.

Mignon Emanuel, he reasoned, was a mere human.

3.

He scarcely saw Oliver for the next few days. This was particularly terrifying, as Myron well knew that he was now in Oliver's power—Oliver knew his plan, or a fictitious but still damning version of it, after all, and furthermore might be completely insane.

By this point in his stay at the house, Myron hardly needed a guide, but Dr. Aluys nevertheless slipped easily and abruptly into the role Oliver had filled. He was often waiting for Myron in the morning when he came down the stairs, and they lunched together in the kitchen. Presumably, Mignon Emanuel wanted someone to keep an eye on him, and Oliver was not reliable enough anymore.

But Myron liked Dr. Aluys. He was a terrific liar, but Myron had become something of one lately, too, so he did not begrudge him this foible. Dr. Aluys, by his own account, had been born near Paris in 1704. His stepfather had taught him the rudiments of alchemy, and it was to this science that he ascribed both his preternaturally long life and his current occupation here.

"The fabrication of the gold, *vraiment,* is not very profitable, believe it or not, by reason of the length of time required in transmutation; of the impossibility of working with amounts more than minute in one time; and indeed by reason of expense of materials required. Nevertheless, it offers something, and something is more than nothing, *non?* In exchange for a certain quantity produced, and a promise I will work to repair Madame Emanuel, I am given my own laboratory, for my own personal research in curing the 'English disease.' Here is where I eat my dinner the most of days."

Myron could not help calling him on this fib. "I've been in your laboratory, and it was covered in cobwebs," he said.

"*Ridicule!*" exclaimed the alchemist. And then, slapping the back of his hand to his forehead, which gesture shot a cloud of powder from his hair, he cried, "*L'alligatâne!*" This, Myron learned later, meant "Alligator-donkey." Dr. Aluys scurried off, returning an hour later covered in what proved to be chickens' blood.

"Fortunately, the alligator can survive of months without alimentation, and his mouth is an alligator's mouth!" Dr. Aluys said, smiling. Turned out he had more than one laboratory. Myron assumed the good doctor had been contracted to treat Mignon Emanuel's platypus venom.

Oh, Dr. Aluys knew all about the conference, but he seemed unconcerned about what it meant. His sole interest, he said, was science, although clearly snuff should have been included on the list. He brought Myron to one of his underground labs and showed him the half-powdered fragments of the philosopher's stone. He also had terrariums with several species of onycophore—what is commonly called the velvet worm. These were small creatures that looked like worms with innumerable nubby legs on which they stalked their prey before snaring it in slime shot out of the face. Dr.

Aluys's delight, as he witnessed, with Myron, the rare *Peripatopsis leonine* catching with slime a grasshopper in midleap, was so intense that Myron felt a little embarrassed for him. But he told the good doctor the story of the snake, the frog, and the parasitic worm, and Dr. Aluys in response danced a little jig on his ancient sticklike legs.

Oh, he could discourse wittily on any topic, but favored, in addition to natural philosophy: dueling, baroque architecture, and décolletage.

"I have a hypothesis subject to you," he told Myron. "Look at your carriage. You march so lightly now, you must be something large when you finally transform. I think you are a mammoth, trapped for of eons in the ice and only now thawed out."

For a moment, Myron was about to say that made pretty good sense. But then he remembered that he was the chosen one. Or, at the very least, if he wasn't, he had to pretend he was the chosen one a little bit longer.

"I'm the chosen one."

"'Tis just a hypothesis."

The doctor, Myron noted, clearly believed Mignon Emanuel was the raccoon she claimed she was, and he wondered if he should disabuse him of this notion. But who knew if he could trust a three-hundred-year-old alchemist?

For that matter, if Mignon Emanuel was not immortal, perhaps only alchemy could explain her youth across the decades.

Dr. Aluys was there when Mrs. Wangenstein brought back from town a black suit for Myron, fitted precisely to his measurements. He was there when Mignon Emanuel coached Myron on the inspirational speech she'd written for him. He had a knack, learned in the courts of kings, doubtless, of loitering almost forgotten in a corner and then suddenly materializing when needed. It made him a congenial companion, and the days before the conference passed quickly. Myron realized at some point that he had been either under observation or in his tower room almost the whole time he'd been in the big house; but he liked having Dr. Aluys around anyway.

It was the first guests at the conference that finally drove the doctor away, back, presumably, to his underground labs. The Central Anarchist Council showed up to the conference twenty hours early, and not at the front but at the kitchen door. There were four of them, and they were very excited that they had managed to slip past the sentries, who had apparently left their posts to chase a strange man with a bow through the woods.

The Central Anarchist Council was excited. There was supposed to be some big, earth-shattering announcement at the conference, and that's why everyone was showing up, but they had their own agenda, they told Myron and Dr. Aluys as they both ate peanut butter and honey sandwiches at the kitchen counter. "In Sèvres, France," the CAC explained, "they have the prototype meter bar—that's the platinum bar that shows the official length of a meter. What we'll do while we're here, we'll get everyone to agree to go to Paris and destroy the meter bar. After that, no one will know how long anything is! No one will be able to measure anything ever again!"

"Non! Non! Le prototype du mètre!" cried Dr. Aluys, and he ran out of the room.

Myron didn't see what all the fuss was about. No one ever used meters, anyway. But he was sorry it had upset Dr. Aluys, whom he never saw, incidentally, again. Finally Florence came into the kitchen to show the Central Anarchist Council to their rooms.

"Where's Oliver?" Myron asked her.

"I think he's in the billiard room," Florence answered absently.

The Central Anarchist Council left behind several empty cans of spray paint, and a tube of airplane glue, which one returned to the kitchen a few minutes later to collect.

"Say, are you Myron?" he asked Myron.

Myron was.

"Man, Gloria wasn't exaggerating about you." He had seen Gloria, it turned out, in Chicago last month. She had refused to come along to the conference. "She used to be a legend; but now she's never up for anything."

Myron finished his sandwich and went to look for Oliver. He walked through the grand ballroom, where tough men dressed in camouflage were hanging up a banner, WELCOME,

DELEGATES. He walked along the tables, noting the engraved nameplates. The Knights of Columbus. The Branch Davidians. The Wallenbergians. The Free Shriners. The Society of the Nights of Eternal Levity. The Carbonari. The Erisians. The National Organization of the Anvil. The Brotherhood of Moloch. The Gormogons. The AFL-CIO. There were no Rosicrucians, of course. There was also no Oliver, wherever Myron looked.

Myron went upstairs to the tower, glanced over his speech, folded it up, and, putting it in the pocket of his suit coat, tried for a long time to go to sleep.

He woke up late. Everyone was too busy to bother with Myron. When he went downstairs, he found that the house was, for once, bustling. Militiamen were running around with clipboards and extension cords. He was suited up and ready, but, of course, unless he found Oliver, nothing would go right. He looked out at the obstacle course, but before he could step outside, Mrs. Wangenstein seized his shoulder.

"The suit must not be permitted to get dirty," she said.

Myron worried that, when he claimed the speech was lost, Mignon Emanuel would somehow know it was in his pocket, and regretted ever bringing it out of his room. He went to the giant vase, peeked inside on tiptoe. His cardboard tube doomsday device was still there. He dropped the speech in as well. It was as good a hiding place as any.

And then he went to every other secret hiding place he knew, but there was no sign of Oliver. Myron began to get the feeling that Oliver had kept some of his best secrets to himself.

By late afternoon, the grand ballroom was beginning to fill up with delegates. Myron peeked in from behind a rear curtain. He wondered if he should just forget all his furtive plans and get swept up in the conference, in the role he could still pretend to play. So many people had shown up, anxious for the promised revelation that was to be his debut. There were the Oddfellows, the Skull and Bones, the pitiful remnant of the Manson Family, the Order of the Harmonious Fist, the Assassins with their homemade bongs, the Kagaali with long beards grinding their sampo, the ATF, three of the Four Tops, the Woman's Christian Temperance Union, the Illuminati—one of the Illuminati saw Myron and waved at him. The man did not have a hand but a metal hook. He tipped his hat up, and Myron recognized Fred "Weishaupt" Meyers. He waved back. He wished he could go talk to him, ask him what happened that day in the Village after he left, but already one of the delegates was standing up and talking. His nameplate identified him as a Wallenbergian.

"Ladies and gentlemen," the man said, a slight lilt in his accent, "let us see if, before we begin, we are able to agree on our agenda for being here."

"Blood for the blood god!" cried the Brotherhood of Moloch in unison.

"Come now," objected one of the Central Anarchist Council. "There is a posted agenda for this conference. Why don't we stick to that?"

The Wallenbergian said, "I'm not competing with the posted agenda. I just want to see if we can agree on certain points *before* the conference starts."

Myron felt a prickling on his neck, and suddenly Mignon Emanuel was behind him. "The Wallenbergians always try to hijack things for their own devices," she whispered in his ear. "I never should have invited them, except they have become so powerful politically."

Myron turned around. Mignon Emanuel was dressed in her finest gray shirt and blazer. It was exactly what she wore every day, except Mrs. Wangenstein had informed Myron earlier that it was much more expensive. For a moment, the tingle on his neck made Myron doubt all his conclusions about Mignon Emanuel—but then he noticed that riding on Mignon's shoulder was a ring-tailed lemur, a handkerchief knotted around something on a thong around its neck.

"Who are the Wallenbergians?" Myron whispered back.

"They are a society that believes that Raoul Wallenberg is a prisoner in Siberia, and seeks his release. They have to bring it up every time, everywhere they go."

"Who's Raoul Wallenberg?" Myron whispered. He felt frustrated to see how little he knew about the groups at the conference, about how little he knew about this world. But there were other things he had to learn than would be taught to him here.

"The greatest human since Chinese Gordon," Mignon Emanuel said. "But still just a human." And then she was called away by an electrical fire.

"Actually, I have a slightly different suggestion about what we should do," the Aum Shinrikyo delegate was saying.

Something grabbed Myron violently from behind. It was Oliver, in a panic. "There you are!" he hissed.

"I've been looking all over for you," Myron said.

"I couldn't come anywhere near you while Miss Emanuel was around. If she saw us together, everything would be ruined." Oliver was shaking, and he looked like death, but, to be fair, Myron hadn't thought of this angle, and he couldn't really argue with the reasoning. "Did you get rid of Florence? You said you would. I didn't see her around."

Myron had to bite his tongue, for he was about to say where Florence really was. It didn't matter, though. Mignon Emanuel would never send Florence to the office while Myron was around, not if she wanted to keep the secret that she was just a human herself. "She'll be gone for a while," he said. "Now let me go tell Miss Emanuel I forgot my speech, and you come up and mention you slipped it under her door, okay?" Oliver did not look very stable or rational at the moment, and Myron was afraid he might have forgotten the plan already.

"Wait," said Oliver. "Give me the speech first, and I'll go stick it under the door."

"You don't have to really slip it under her door, it's a lie. A ruse. Just say you did."

"But what if she checks? She'll know I lied."

"How will she check? If she goes there later, we can just say we picked it up. It doesn't matter."

"It definitely matters, just give me that speech."

Myron was holding his head. "I don't have it on me anymore."

"Tell me where it is. I'll go get it."

"Oliver, we don't have time! Just pretend you put it under the door."

"Don't be an idiot, where did you hide it?"

Finally, Myron told him about the vase. As soon as Oliver left, Myron regretted that he had not gone himself. What would he do if Mignon Emanuel made him go out before Oliver came back? It wasn't far to the vase, of course, but who knew what Oliver would do, once out of Myron's sight? He peeked again, through the curtain, at the scene on the ballroom floor, but his sight was blocked by the Knights of Columbus delegates, who were standing and administering to each other, in a ring, their traditional oath: "I will go to any part of the world whithersoever I may be sent, to the frozen regions north, jungles of India, to the centers of civilization of Europe, or to the wild haunts of the barbarous savages of America without murmuring or repining . . ." It went on and on, and Myron couldn't tell what was happening beyond them. He kept checking his watch nervously, but he wasn't wearing a watch, so instead he just kept lifting his left arm halfway to his face like a crazy person. When the Knights of Columbus sat, the rest of the delegates began to stomp their feet in impatience.

And then he felt Florence, and therefore Mignon Emanuel, coming up behind him. "Are you almost ready for showtime, Myron?" Mignon Emanuel asked with an encouraging smile.

The stomping grew louder. *Where the deuce was Oliver?* "Er," Myron said, stalling for time. "Actually, well, this is embarrassing to say, but, actually"—he was stuck halfway through the sentence, and had nowhere to go but forward—"it turns out I can't find the speech."

"What?" Mignon Emanuel snapped.

"I really need it. Do you have another copy?" And for a moment of sheer terror he wondered what he would do if she did have one. He hadn't prepared for one moment to get in front of the delegation. He had only a cursory idea of what he was even supposed to say. The incredible fear somehow managed to increase.

"Oh, I saw that in the hall," Oliver said, arriving from nowhere. Myron noticed with alarm that he had the cardboard tube held casually behind his back. "I slid it under your office door, I thought it was yours."

Mignon Emanuel looked from Myron to Oliver and back.

"I recognized your handwriting, so I figured it belonged to you," Oliver continued, as Myron tried to will him into shutting up.

Mignon Emanuel now turned her full attention on Oliver.

"I mean your typewriting," he said.

Myron managed to croak out, "Maybe one of us should go get it."

The stomping of the restless crowd was reaching a fever pitch. Mignon turned to Oliver. He was sweating profusely, and swaying a little. "If we must," she said, with her most chilling voice. It was not a dark and forgotten tongue, but it scared the hell out of Myron nevertheless. She pulled a key ring out of her breast pocket, carefully sliding one key off it; she went to hand it to Oliver, and then, with a sideways glance at the lemur on her shoulder, changed her mind. "Myron, I'll take my time on the introductory remarks," she said, handing him the key. "For God's sake, don't tarry, and don't mess up your speech. There is a lot riding on this for both of us. For both of us." And Myron was off at a run. He stopped when applause told him that Mignon Emanuel had stepped onto the ballroom floor. Turning around, he caught Oliver's eye and gestured at the tube. *Give it to me.* Oliver smiled and shook his head. With his free hand he described a shape in the air. Myron nodded and, leaving Oliver behind, began to run again.

He ran down the hall, past burly men stacking hors d'oeuvres and loosening champagne corks. Around the corner with the Heppelwhite serpentine chest, and down the long green carpet, and there before him was the office door. He fumbled with and dropped the key before he managed to shoot the bolt. He practically fell into the room. It was dark, but motion detectors activated the small reading light on the desk. There on the floor in front of him were the pages of his speech. Myron realized that it shouldn't have been so dark, since it was still dusk, and looked up at the skylight, but the skylight was covered with an opaque screen. He wasted a few precious seconds looking for a switch to retract the screen, for better lighting, and then gave up and opened the top drawer of the desk. Inside was a small key. He used it to open the large drawer, and from inside that, under some juggling clubs, a dismantled Bunsen burner, a signed baseball (signed, I have reason to believe, by the 1919 Chicago White Sox), a railroad lantern, and a jade elephant with a clock on its back, he pulled a ring of six ancient keys. He didn't *really* know whether the keys would open the door; he didn't *really* know what kind of doomsday device would be behind the door. But he had seen the look on Mignon Emanuel's face when he mentioned the room, and he knew that his studies, his messiahship, his comfortable life here in the big house—it was worth throwing all of these away for one look in Pandora's box.

There were other plans competing for a place on his agenda—perhaps he should look for the promised sliding bookshelf, perhaps he should go through the locked cabinet in the wall, perhaps he should be rummaging through the desk or even just picking up a juggling club in case he had to brain Oliver to get the tube back—but they all got tabled, and Myron was sprinting for the door. He felt his neck prickle just as he saw something cat-size jump down across the doorway, and there, standing up from a crouch on the ground, was Florence.

"You forgot the speech," she said, stepping forward over the pages.

Myron felt, along with everything else, extremely uncomfortable because she was naked. "I don't want to hurt you," he said, perhaps wishing he had taken the club after all.

"You won't."

I have hitherto failed to belabor the unfortunate truth, which the perspicacious reader will already have appertained: that Myron was in fact shorter than Florence. She outweighed him, as well, and had a superior reach. She was unconstricted by a Fauntleroy three-piece suit. There was every reason to assume she was the stronger, too. Myron, in desperation, tried—if it had been a punch, it would have been a pretty sissy punch, but really it was a just a one-handed push. Florence quickly shifted her weight, and Myron went right past her. He thought for a moment he was home free, but then she kicked him in the back of the knee and he went down. She jumped on his back and pinned his shoulders with her hands. He was lying half on, half off the tiger-skin rug.

"Emanuel will be here soon," she said. "Just relax and wait it out."

Myron gasped something out—"Tapeworm," it sounded like. He flailed his arms backwards, trying desperately to claw at Florence. She easily avoided the clumsy attempt, of course, but then Myron gave a particularly mighty heave, straining the arm in the socket, and his hand slipped up through the leather thong Florence had around her neck. Florence jerked backwards, but the thong was caught on his wrist, and she couldn't pull away.

At first Myron thought Florence has seized his hand in some kind of judo wristlock, and was just torturing him. But in trying to escape the hold he wrapped the thong around his wrist again, and the biting of the thong into his flesh was a distinctive enough sensation that Myron caught on and repeated the motion. He moved his arm in a circle until the thong was wound painfully tight around his forearm. He could hear Florence gagging behind him. Suddenly the weight was off him, and there was a moment of crisis, as a lemur attempted to draw its tiny head through the loop; but Myron jerked his arm forward, bringing the small creature with it, and he was able to use his other hand to tighten the noose. The lemur scratched, but she could not bite him, and her scratches were feeble. Then she tried to turn into a human again, but that was a bad idea—her throat was too large, and the constriction must have been terrible. She managed to get on top of his prone body, and grabbed his face with her hands and went for his eyes, but before she got any further she grew limp and fell forward, onto Myron's head.

Myron slithered out from underneath her. He carefully unwrapped the thong from his arm and her throat. The knotted handkerchief on the thong, he removed it to confirm that the shape was there. When he left Florence breathing shallowly, in one pocket he had the shape, in the other the key ring. His arm was bleeding in several places, and his hand was slowly fading from purple.

And he was running again, back toward the room. He took a detour through the defunct pinball arcade to avoid passing right by the grand ballroom. He wasn't taking any risks.

The first key he tried, when he reached the forbidden door, didn't fit the lock, and the second one was too small and rattled around inside the keyhole. The third one slipped in partway, got stuck, and then with a rip slid home. It fit snug, but before Myron could turn it, a wave of nausea and confusion washed over him. He shook it off and, as he took a deep breath and steeled himself, he heard a voice down the corridor: "Don't open that door."

To no one's surprise it was Mignon Emanuel, striding slowly and purposefully, with Oliver scurrying along ahead of her. Oliver ran right past Myron and kept going, but Mignon Emanuel stopped a few yards away when she saw that Myron had the key poised for turning.

"Please, Myron. The conference is waiting for you. For you!"

Suddenly Myron began to cry. "You lied to me! You're not even one of us."

"I am one of you."

"I can tell, I can tell who is and who isn't. Don't lie to me. You're not."

"I knew I sensed something, you followed me the other day—Myron, I am one of you, I promise you. This is my trick. I figured out a way to hide the scent, so no one could tell I was around. Benson's the only one who knew I could do it, Benson and Florence now; but I tried it too often and it got stuck. That's when I left Marcus—I didn't want him to know I could do it. I'm trying to get it back where I can turn it on and off. You've got to believe me." Her face was contorted in desperation and agony, and she held her hand out. "I have so many plans for us. Please, Myron, come back to the conference."

"Okay, prove it, then. Turn into a raccoon."

"I can't. I told you, the platypus—"

"I don't believe you! I don't even believe platypuses are poisonous!"

Mignon Emanuel said, "Venomou—"

But at that moment there was an explosion, somewhere off in the house. The foundation shook. There were screams in the distance, delegates shouting and stampeding. The abrupt crackling of flames. Mignon Emanuel paused mid-word, and turned her head toward the noise. And Myron turned the key and pushed the door open.

The swinging of the door triggered the motion detector, and the light went on in the room. Exhaust fans were already running. The floor was ornately tiled, and the tiles spelled out a motto in Latin, which of course Myron could not read, but I have it on no less an authority than Dr. Aluys's, who survived the incident and whom I later interviewed, that it was a quote from Emperor Vespatian, who said to his subjects on his deathbed (and I translate), "Why do you weep? Did you think I was immortal?" The walls, somewhat less tastefully, were covered with tinfoil, as was, Myron could only suppose, the back of the door, including the keyhole he had popped through. Tinfoil over the keyhole (his mind was working rapidly) could have been pinpricked by Oliver when he tried to pick the lock, and would explain why, when it was reapplied, Myron could no longer smell the room beyond. But none of this was what was surprising.

All along the walls of the room, like a hunting lodge's, were the heads of animals, mounted on plaques: a bighorn sheep, a beaver, a wolverine, a caribou, and so on. Smaller plaques held the whole bodies of stuffed rodents and rabbits. In the center of the room was a nearly complete skeleton of a great cat, bound together with silver wire, its right foreleg missing. And then Myron realized that this was not a bighorn sheep or a beaver, this was *the* bighorn sheep and *the* beaver; because there, there newly mounted to one side of the door, there was the moose. He had died with no antlers, of course, so the taxidermist had provided him with false antlers, but they were a cruel mockery of the antlers Myron remembered, these were stunted, misshapen devil's antlers falsely wired to his great head. The bile rising in his stomach, his head still swimming, Myron, who had taken all of this in during a mere moment, turned back in wrath to Mignon

Emanuel. He screamed, and she—she was occluded by the shredded, floating remains of a twenty-five-hundred-dollar outfit. And then, standing in her place, roaring and eight feet tall, was a bear.

Myron thought he was going to die. But the bear turned away from him and batted with an enormous paw something fast and on fire. The fiery bolt crashed into a wall, blasting a hole in it. Past the bear, standing amid the smoke and flame, Myron could now see a young Indian man with a bow, an arrow nocked in it. The arrow appeared to be shimmering, or pulsating, strangely.

"Get away—he's mine!" the young man shouted. He was, of course, Myron perceived, the man he had fought among the Nine Unknown Men in New York.

The bear became Mignon Emanuel again. "You're not going to hurt him."

"I only want to hurt him for a few minutes," said the man, whose name, Myron had finally put together, must be Dantaghata. "Then I'll kill him."

"Don't be absurd," said Mignon Emanuel. "You know you can't kill us."

"Are you certain?" Dantaghata said. "I hold the Pashupatastra, unmaker of worlds, the irresistible weapon of Lord Shiva the Destroyer."

Mignon Emanuel blanched. Myron could not see her face, so he could not see if she looked afraid, but her voice betrayed her when she asked, "Is that . . . is that arrow there the Pashupatastra?"

"Of course not—the Pashupatastra is reserved for him. But this is the Narayanastra."

"Oh, is that all?" said Mignon Emanuel with relief, and became a bear, charging down the corridor at the archer.

Myron immediately turned the other way and ran smack into Oliver. He pushed the larger boy out of the way and then pulled him as they ran around a corner.

"That was the most amazing thing I've ever seen," Oliver said.

Myron said nothing.

"Did you see that?" Oliver asked. "Miss Emanuel was *naked*."

"Come along," Myron said.

They ran a while longer—it was a big house. Oliver said, along the way, that he thought Mignon Emanuel might have followed him to the rendezvous at the locked door. Myron didn't have the strength to remind him that there had been no rendezvous. The sounds of thunderclaps echoed along the corridors. Finally they reached a back door to the outside, and Myron turned to Oliver and said, "I'm going to go to the West Coast. I'm going to go looking for the Rosicrucians."

"Wait, you want to *leave?*"

"I don't know who else might even know about what's going on. Look, maybe you should come, too. We can look for your parents, they're near there, right?"

"You can't go, you were just starting to be cool!"

"Oliver, you don't belong here. These people are crazy,

and they're liars, and, Oliver, they kill people. We've got to go."

But stretching up to his full height, Oliver scoffed, "Yeah, well, good luck getting anywhere without your poster tube."

So Myron handed over the shape and then, when Oliver fell over and curled up fetal around it, picked up the cardboard tube he had dropped. Leaving Oliver, and everything, behind, Myron ran across the lawn, doubling around to pick up his bow from the side of the obstacle course where it had been abandoned on the wet ground. It was already dark, and it was getting darker. Then he was off, into the pitch-black woods.

One quick last glance back to confirm that the house was on fire, and in places beginning to collapse.

VIII

On the C

When you say I am a thief, Pete, you lie. You can kill me, but still I will say you lie.

Jack London, *The Cruise of the "Dazzler"*

I.

There is a famous paradox, probably already familiar to you from the letters of Paul: Epimenides the Cretan has stated that all Cretans are liars. But if Cretans are liars, who trusts Epimenides the Cretan when he tells us all Cretans are liars? If you are a space robot, your circuits have already been fried by reading this.

Slightly less well-known is the fact that Plato, who proclaimed that all poets are liars, was himself a poet. "I wish I were the night, so I could watch you sleep with its thousand eyes," he wrote. In Greek it's a poem. Plato was therefore a liar.

Or was he? I mention Plato in the first place because he also proposed, through the mouth of Socrates, that so-called learning is merely recollecting what we, or our immortal souls, already knew. Usually this, like much Platonism, sounds spurious to me—Plato also said that humans were once four-armed hermaphrodites, and I think I would remember that if it were true—but Myron offers a curious case.

I have written a great many stories in my time, as I have mentioned, and certainly many of them involved a young man learning various things. Myron, at the very least, is or has been an amnesiac. For him, if anyone, learning can be recollection. What did he learn in the Fortress of the Id (as I call it)? Or what did he recall there? As he was leaving, dashing through the woods, did he think he was wiser than he had been two months before? Did he think he was as wise as he had been ten years before?

To be handed, after years or even a lifetime of powerlessness, a chance at power, this must be a heady feeling. But Myron had lost it, and whether he had thrown it away in the pursuit of absolute truth, or whether it had been wrenched from his grasp by a capricious fate—well, it was probably a little of both. The woods were cold and filled with burrs, and Myron was alone. For a good twenty feet the dim light from the blaze lit his way, and then abruptly it was dark. Whatever tears he shed in the blackness may have been for Spenser and may have been for himself.

When he finally stumbled onto a highway, his fancy suit was in rags and he was covered in mud. He kept his head down and stuck his thumb out. He asked the first trucker who picked him up if he was headed for the West Coast, but this was, of course, the wrong road for that. They were going to Chicago, which, Myron said, was good enough. Frankly, it was the only place he knew where someone he knew was.

Over the next two hundred and fifty miles, Myron passed the time inventing stories about how he had gotten separated from his Chicagoan family and cleaning himself with several-dozen premoistened towelettes. "I can give myself a complete bath with those things and still keep one hand on the wheel," his driver said. "Wanna see?" But Myron faked asleep, and soon he really was.

Once within Chicago city limits, Myron hopped out at a stoplight and ran the wrong way up a one-way street, leaving behind only his hastily shouted thanks. Then he just looked up the Central Anarchist Council in a phone book. He went to the address and claimed he had burned his face off with acid protesting the existence of the bourgeoisie. The guy he was talking to didn't know what the bourgeoisie was, but he thought burning your face off with acid was pretty hard-core, and he just went ahead and told Myron where to find Gloria. At a bowling alley, passed out in a booth near the back. She was wearing a powder blue tracksuit, with a unicorn on the top. Her shoes were not regulation. Half a cigarette had smoldered out in her hand. As Myron slid in across from her, Gloria's head snapped up.

"Hello," he said.

Gloria said nothing.

"I want to go to the West Coast to meet the Rosicrucians," Myron said. "But I have no idea where they are, and I have no way of getting there. Can you help me?"

"Follow me," said Gloria, lighting another cigarette.

They went out a back door into an alley. "Tie your shoe," Gloria said. She held the doomsday device and the compound bow while Myron bent over. When he straightened up again, Gloria was atop a fire escape, her clothes a little disheveled. She was looking at the cardboard tube with doomsday inside it.

"Actually, I don't want this," she said, and dropped it down to Myron, who caught it after some bobbling.

"Hey, come back with my bow," Myron then said.

"No one knows where the Rosicrucians are," Gloria said. "You should probably just ask the Nine Unknown Men."

"They want to kill me," Myron said.

"They do, huh? You're better at this than I thought."

"Give me back my bow."

"I' faith, Myron, I'm doing this to teach you a valuable lesson about the world. No one else is going to take the time to teach you these things—"

Myron shouted up, interrupting, "Mignon Emanuel gave me lessons all the time."

"She did? Like what?"

"Like about confirmation bias."

"What the devil is that?"

"That's when you notice things that agree with what you already believe more often than things that contradict your beliefs."

"I've never noticed anything of the sort. Anyway, she

was just using you, I heard all about the conference. No one else—"

"Spenser taught me all about woodcraft. He taught me how to make a fire with a soda can, and how to build a shelter."

"The moose taught you how to build a fire?"

"And he taught me all about the lycanthropes, and how there's one of each species and everything."

"No, I taught you that. I taught you that in Shoreditch."

"Well, he taught me more, about the Time of Troubles, and who killed who."

"That was all implicit in what I told you," Gloria shouted down. "You could have pieced it together yourself."

"And he told me about meeting you in Scotland."

"I had no way of knowing you'd even be interested in that."

"And he taught me how things always get worse."

"I could have told you that! Did you think I couldn't have told you that?"

"I don't know."

"Marry! I'll show you what I know." Gloria turned, up on the fire escape, from an old woman into a gorilla. Her clothes stretched out but stayed on the gorilla; they just fit poorly. A cigarette still dangled from her lips. She jumped down to the alleyway and then became a woman again. The tracksuit was bunched up at the knee and off kilter around the shoulders. "No Unknown Men, then," she said. "Some of us have met the Rosicrucians, although there are only three that I know of still alive. The lion's one, but he's right out. There's the ring-tailed lemur."

"I strangled her unconscious, and then her house blew up. Also, I don't think she likes me."

"Her house blew up? You are better at this than I'd thought. Well, that leaves the coyote."

"And you'll tell me where the coyote is?"

"Oh, Myron, that's not what I'm going to teach you. I'm going to teach you so much more. You're going to learn life on the C."

On the sea was not something Myron had expected to hear in Chicago, and he had a bout of excitement mixed with a minor panic attack that his knowledge of geography was totally kinked. But the *C* was for *con*.

"I would really prefer not to steal from anyone," Myron objected.

"What about when you liberated that suit of clothes in Shoreditch?"

"I was going to freeze to death! I needed that suit of clothes, and it was an emergency!" Looking back, Myron wasn't sure this was true. He had been awfully cavalier about the theft.

"Well, we're not even going to steal anything at all. We're going to persuade people to give us stuff. It's the only way we'll be able to find the Rosicrucians. And anyway, we'll be like Robin Hood, or some romantic jewel thief. We'll only steal from the rich, and they can afford it."

Myron was skeptical, but desperate. "Only from the rich?"

"The haute bourgeoisie only."

But this, too, turned out to be a lie.

2.

The first thing Myron needed was a suit of clothes—the current one was unsalvageable, but he didn't need anything that nice, really. Just anything that had not dashed through the muddy, thorny woods at night.

The bow and tube Gloria stashed at the bowling alley, under a ceiling panel in the ladies' room. Then, on the bus ride out to the purlieus along Kimbark Avenue, she smoked incessantly and explained to Myron the basic tenet of life on the C. You simply (she said) had to be absolutely certain of everything you say. Most people are rarely absolutely certain, so if you sounded like you know what you were talking about, they would tend to go along with you. Should you ever meet someone else who is absolutely sure, apologize for the mistake and leave. This person is probably too stupid to fool and may be extremely dangerous.

The bus let them off in a quiet residential neighborhood. Two streets over they came to a small children's-clothing store—but they didn't go in. Leaving Myron outside, Gloria went to the bagel shop next door and came out empty-handed.

"I am pretty hungry," Myron said.

"There'll be time for that later, we're working. I went in there and asked for one hundred and ninety-nine onion bagels. The woman was surprised, and she asked me why I didn't order two hundred. I said, Are you crazy? Who can eat two hundred bagels? Then we both laughed. So you get it?"

"Yeah, I guess," Myron said.

"This way, when I say, sure, give me two hundred bagels, she can't object—it was practically her idea. I told her I was going to be dropping them off at various local businesses as part of a charity drive. Now I sound like a mensch. She just told me to come back in a couple of hours, with the understanding that I would pay on delivery. Do you follow it so far? Now to look at suits."

They spent a long time in the clothing store. The proprietor was an old man who drew a sharp intake of breath when he saw Myron, but Gloria quickly explained that "boys be boys," and she needed new church clothes for her grandson. Myron did look a fright; he always looked a fright, but this was something special. He had to be careful not to touch any of the suits, lest he get mud on them, but Gloria held them up in front of him to eyeball a size. The suit and a new shirt were priced at almost a hundred dollars, and Myron warned her in a whisper that he had no money.

"You don't need money when you're on the C. This is what you have to do. When I open the door, you run out, go next door to the bagel shop, and open the door;

catch the woman's eye and then leave. She should step out-side after you—it's important she step outside. Can you do that?"

They brought their selection to the front counter, and the man rang them up and boxed the ensemble, nestled in tissue paper.

"I done forget my wallet," Gloria said, tucking the box beneath her arm. "You mind if it go on my account?" She took a step to the right and opened the door, and Myron darted out.

The proprietor looked worried, and he stepped out from behind the counter. "Ma'am, I don't mean nothing by it, but I don't know you. I never seen you before. You don't have no account here, and I hope I don't sound suspicious if I say so." As he opened the door to the bagel shop, Myron could hear the man saying something more or less like this. And there in the bagel shop the woman gasped at the sight of this tiny revenant, and came running out after Myron, who was backpedaling.

And so, at that moment, Gloria stood in the open door of the clothing store, its proprietor a half step behind her, and the bagel seller a few feet to her right. The three of them made almost a straight line, with Myron the anoma-lous point, floating away backwards into the parking lot. It was at the moment that Gloria took control of the situation. Turning to the bagel woman, she said, "When you have two hundred for me, honey?"

Surprised, the woman said she needed another hour or two.

"Well, make sure he get one hundred, will you?" Gloria said. Then she smiled and nodded at the clothing store proprietor, who could no longer very well object. He was grinning, and the grin was a grin of heartbreaking trust. And as the door dinged shut behind her, Gloria said to the bagel seller, "I'm a come back in an hour."

Gloria gestured Myron over and took him by the hand. The woman returned to her bagels. Myron and Gloria walked away. They hopped on the first bus they saw.

"That was called the Laurie, after Joe Laurie, who invented it," Gloria lectured.

"What's that woman going to do with two hundred onion bagels?" Myron asked. "What's that man going to do when he figures it all out?"

"You did a good job today. Now we've got to get you cleaned up."

Gloria was currently staying in an abandoned and crumbling building. To get to her section of the building you had to pass over a part with no floor. Gloria as a gorilla could go hand over hand above the hole, but Myron could only nervously balance his way across a narrow beam. On the far side, Myron got washed in a basin of rainwater, and Gloria put on a bright orange muumuu.

"You put on loose clothes and hope they'll work with the change," she complained, "and it almost all works except for the underthings."

They cleaned off Myron's shoes, Gloria fashioned fake socks (she'd forgotten to get socks!) out of the pieces of his vest that had not been soiled, and, after a quick amateur haircut, Myron was presentable. "Now let's go see what we can find out."

With the speed of a montage, they went on a whirlwind tour of retirement communities in Chicago and environs. The plan was Gloria's. Myron would go in the front. Usually he could just duck under the front desk and no one noticed him, but if they noticed him, and didn't ignore him under the assumption that he was someone's renegade grandson, one look at his face usually shut them up long enough for him to get away; now that he was well groomed, and it was clear his face was not the result of a raw wound but was actually stuck that way, they were just too embarrassed to stop him. Then Myron would hasten to a rear fire door and let Gloria in. That was his only job, and sometimes he would slip out as she slipped in, to meet up with her later; but sometimes he would stick around to learn. Gloria would go to the rec room, pretend to be new here, find three more for bridge, and after losing a few rubbers, say, "Well, we could continue to play for pennies, but why don't we make this next rubber *interesting?*"

Basically, she cheated old people at cards. Myron didn't see how this helped him, but she did, on occasion, ask her partner casually about a particular canine fellow. Angel Sanchez, his name might be, or Hussein El-Agale, or Jack Thompson. On street corners, she'd approach a news vendor, or a prostitute, and make a casual inquiry. Days went by. The doomsday device and Myron's precious bow were moved to a more secure hiding place. She and Myron ate well, and the squatter's quarters Gloria favored were surprisingly warm and even cozy. But there was no sign of any coyote.

Myron was practically writhing in frustration at the delay. "Maybe you shouldn't go see the Rosicrucians after all, maybe you should just live life on the C," Gloria suggested. But Myron was adamant. He had no reason to trust the Rosicrucians; but the fact that he had no reason to distrust them made them, he maintained, unique in all the world. Gloria sniffed at his answer and launched into another lecture.

Because Gloria lectured Myron, incessantly, especially on how there was no point in lecturing anyone. *The only true propaganda was propaganda by the deed.* As far as Myron could tell, propaganda by the deed meant doing whatever jerky stuff you felt like doing. "'There are no innocent bourgeois,'" Gloria said, quoting Emil Henry, who had been guillotined by the French government in 1894 merely because he was a murderer and a terrorist.

"'The advocates of a criminal are seldom artists enough to turn the beautiful terribleness of the deed to the advantage of the doer,'" she added, quoting Nietzsche. And she shook her fist, at the world, over the tragic fate of Emil Henry.

"Did you know Nietzsche was murdered," Myron said, "by the flying squirrel?"

"That's just an urban legend," Gloria said. Her eyes were blazing with fire. When they started to blaze, Myron knew he was not going to get a lot from her. But at other times her advice was useful. She taught him to watch, at cards, for people's *tells*, little twitches or gestures that would reveal their hand. She also taught him how to read cards in the re-flections in people's glasses, and switch decks while pretend-ing to cut.

And watching her he learned how to change his dialect to fit in with whomever he was talking to. No matter what animal you were, Gloria explained, to get along you also had to be a chameleon.

They went to the library, purportedly to follow a lead about Angel Sanchez, but probably, Myron suspected, just to look up where there were more old folks' homes. Gloria pointed out to Myron a hand-lettered sign on the wall. NO GUM CHEWING ALLOWED.

"So?" Myron asked. "That makes sense. People might put gum under the tables, or in a book."

"So why don't they just make a rule that you're not al-lowed to put gum under the tables? Why do they ban gum altogether?"

"Well, it's hard to catch people sticking gum somewhere. It's much easier to catch them chewing it."

Gloria nodded. "That's very important. Most rules are there not to help you or make your life better but to make things easier for the rule enforcers. Always remember that."

And as soon as she said it, Myron suddenly understood

a lot about his junior high experience. It made a lot more sense now.

"The moose never taught you anything like this," Gloria gloated.

The lead was a dud, of course. Lead after lead was a dud, and the coyote, as coyotes do, remained elusive. They did manage to acquire quite a nest egg, though, and one day Gloria said, "Now I'm going to teach you about the system."

Gloria had never spoken so positively about the system, so Myron was confused. But it turned out Gloria meant her system for betting on the ponies. This system proved flawed, too, and she lost almost all their money in forty-five minutes, and then spent the rest on gin. That night, Myron finally told Gloria that Spenser was dead, and she cried and threw the gin bottle off a rooftop, and then had to go steal a new one. Myron was worried he was getting nowhere.

And one day, as he walked along the back alleys, he felt his neck prickling, and when he looked up, he saw something that might have been a cat leap across the gap between rooftops and then run away. Black and white on its tail. It might not have been a cat. Myron was getting scared.

3.

Of course, Gloria was not really looking for a coyote. She only made inquiries when she knew she'd get a negative response. She only looked for his spoor down alleys she suspected he would never go. Anything to prevent another clue from materializing, while offering the promise of another clue like a rainbow's end, always just at the horizon. I know Gloria, and I know how she works, and she was running the long con. And on the long con, all you need to do is wear your mark down. Myron was tenacious, but perhaps she could have worn him down in time, perhaps she could have gotten him acclimated to life on the C. She had never believed what Myron believed, as he became more and more frightened of the shadows: that time could possibly run out.

Gloria took a lot of risks, frankly, since she was used to dodging the cops and not the lion, or the bear, or me. It's hardly surprising that someone would catch wind of her antics, and one day she telegraphed carelessly what joint she'd hit up next. And so Myron was killing time outside a rest home, while Gloria took advantage inside, when a slim man in a tweed cap came slinking up. He was smoking a cigarette in a long, thin quellazaire. Myron could tell that he was one of us.

"You want to find the coyote, come with me," he said gruffly, trying to grab Myron's arm.

"I don't want to find the coyote," Myron said, twisting away. "I just want to find the Rosicrucians."

"What, the main temple in Portland?"

"Yeah, that one," Myron said.

"The one behind the Twenty-Four-Hour Church of Elvis? Everyone knows where that is, why would you care? Now come on, the coyote's waiting for you."

But Myron turned and ran straight into the rest home. "No running!" shouted the guard. And Myron stopped in the lobby and looked over his shoulder. The slim man was watching him through the glass double doors, and then with a shrug he slunk away.

"No running," said the guard again, trying not to look at Myron's face.

When Gloria turned up again, wearing a strand of pearls she had just won, Myron excitedly told her what had happened. The Rosicrucians were in Portland! Must be Portland, Oregon! All they needed to do was take their winnings and hop a bus!

But Gloria waved him off. "Myron, that fellow was obviously the ermine, and the ermine has never been trustworthy. The whole thing is a trap."

"No, no, I tricked him into revealing the location," Myron insisted.

"You didn't trick him, he was trapping you."

"So the Rosicrucians aren't in Portland?"

"They're probably in Portland. Myron, truth is more dangerous than lies at this point."

"We can go scope the place out at least."

But Gloria had invested all their savings in lottery tickets, which, it turns out, gave them a microscopic chance of being able to travel to the West Coast in a private jet and a very good chance of not being able to afford leaving Chicago at all.

"You said," Myron objected, "that you don't need money

when you're on the C. Why can't you just talk your way onto a bus?" She'd more or less done it before, after all.

But Gloria wanted to wait for the lottery drawing. She said Myron didn't know when he had a good thing. She insisted (against all evidence) that it was safer in Chicago.

"How can it be safer here?" Myron asked. The lion knows we're here."

If Gloria was thinking, *Well, he knows* you're *here,* she was too smart to say it out loud. "I'll tell you what. If one more person gets wise to us, we'll leave."

But she was no more careful than before, and two days later a Volkswagen Bug pulled up next to the two of them as they were trying to hustle a businessman at a bus stop. You should have seen Myron's eyes light up when he saw who was driving.

I was, of course. And that's when his adventures began.

IX

The Adventure Begins

And there was the body—mere flesh and blood, no more—but such flesh, and so much blood!

Charles Dickens, *Oliver Twist*

I.

It will be unnecessary for me to enumerate the tricks and schemes I went through to find Myron. I'd heard a few rumors about Mignon Emanuel's plans, of course, but I'd heard them all too late. And then a friend of a friend of an acquaintance had a tip that led me to a back-alley unlicensed tattoo parlor in Hartford, where Angel Sanchez told me he had learned that Gloria and some "mutant kid" were looking for him. Gloria wasn't answering my calls (I think she had actually lost her phone), and Alice, with her pickup truck and my forty-five, was three thousand miles away—so I borrowed the Bug from Angel "for a day or two" (which was a lie) and drove to Chicago. I didn't find Myron right away, but I found him. It can be a small world, this animal world of ours.

The boy was practically giddy with excitement. We stopped by Gloria's nest to grab Myron's stuff. I noticed that the tape seal had been broken around one end of the doomsday device, but Myron claimed he'd never opened it all the way. I grabbed from the trunk two canvas bags and stashed the device in one, Myron's compound bow in the other. Both ended up on the back seat. I also pulled out my typewriter, a jadeite green Hermes 2000 in a leatherette case. I have a job, naturally—I would never admit it to Myron, but I currently ghostwrite the best-selling Magic Pony Club books—but I was currently behind on more than one deadline, so I'd brought the typewriter to try to catch up on the road, and I stuck it in the back seat, partially in case I needed it and mostly to clutter up the back seat so it would look there was no room for Gloria to come along. Oh, I invited her for appearances' sake, but the answer was never really in question. The adventure was beginning, why bother with the hindrances of the past? She gave Myron a sawbuck and a bit of advice ("Never play cards with an actuary"), also an awkward hug, and we were off. After several unpleasant potholes and a steam grate that was frankly blinding, we entered the long stretch on I-80.

"We're going to Portland," Myron said as we motored west.

"No, we're going to Sacramento to meet Alice," I corrected him. "She has a safe house there."

Myron flipped out. "What? The Rosicrucians are in Portland."

"Maybe they are and maybe they aren't, but you're not going to go meet the Rosicrucians. It's obviously a trap."

He crossed his arms and sulked. I think he might have tried to jump out of the car if we hadn't been speeding. Also, I can assure you that his deep-seated respect for me would have kept him in check.

"This is going to be a long trip," I goaded him, "if no one talks."

But Myron could not stay mad at me for long, though. Who could? Gloria forgave me, Alice time and again forgave me, I'm sure you'll forgive me, too, after the part where you find out and get mad. My crime against Myron, the crime of not driving him directly to his doom, was comparatively minor. And he warmed up eventually.

I tried to help him understand. "Ask me anything," I told him. "You'll be surprised what I know."

Q: Why did Mignon Emanuel's militia guards have harpoon guns?

A: In case any lions showed up, harpoons, and their tangling lines, are better for stopping them than ineffectual bullets.

Q: Why does Gloria talk that way: *i' faith* and *zounds?*

A: You tend to internalize a language best when you first learn it. Gloria learned English sometime in the sixteenth century, so when she gets distracted or excited, she falls upon old habits. In contrast, I learned English from a set of *The History of the Decline and Fall of the Roman Empire* I

acquired from a British soldier in India in 1791,
so my speech, like my prose, is as pellucid as
Edward Gibbon's.

Q: Who was still looking to kill Myron?

A: Too many people to count, now.

Q: Why don't we go see the Rosicrucians?

A: BECAUSE IT'S A TRAP!

Ah, but how did I know it was a trap? The ermine may or may not have been in league with the lion, but he was in league with somebody. And when it came down to it, the Rosicrucians were much more likely to want to help someone as powerful as Mr. Bigshot than our little Myron. And also they were the Rosicrucians. Who trusts them?

Myron was far too trusting. He believed he was paranoid, but he didn't know real paranoia: he couldn't remember the Time of Troubles. I was amazed by how little animosity, though, he had toward Mignon Emanuel and Florence. He actually seemed concerned that Florence was the last survivor of the Vazimba. He also seemed to think I was callous for not sympathizing.

"Her whole people were wiped out! Isn't that sad?"

"Kid," I said, "everybody's whole people were wiped out. You knew Spenser, right?" (I'd heard about Spenser.) "Spenser's from Scotland before the Celts arrived. What do you think the Celts did when they got there? Here's a hint: Scotland ended up Celtic. And anyway, there are plenty of Vazimba left—I've met at least three species of civet, and a fossa—they just don't like Florence. And anyway, the real Vazimba are not Florence's people. The real Vazimba are humans."

But Myron still seemed to care even about Mrs. Wangenstein. She'd been blackmailed a little, by the way, but mostly she'd been bribed. And Oliver, too. "I hope he's okay," Myron said.

"He's alive; he's back with his parents, I'd heard. But I don't think he's okay, if you get what I mean."

It was a long drive, and finally Myron began to tell me his story, much of which I'd already pieced together, fragmentarily and at times inaccurately. "Hold the wheel, will you, I want to take notes," I said. But Myron seemed to think this was dangerous. He wouldn't even let me set my typewriter up while I drove. I tried to explain I was a touch-typist, so it was perfectly safe, but perhaps Myron was notching closer to the paranoid ideal. I couldn't wait until we were able to stop, so I could write things down, but I kept driving, anyway, because I didn't want to break his train of thought. Finally, in a dull generic motel in Grand Island, Nebraska, which is incidentally not an island, I pretended to a desk clerk, who was literally eating paint chips, that Myron was my son. He faced away from the front desk. The warped and filthy key card got us into a room with a bed and a cot. I was tired from driving, but I stayed up till all hours, despite the people who banged on the walls and shouted through the door, typing up what Myron had told me.

Instead of starting out again the next day, I just had him tell me everything again, while I took more notes. I know I also made a note to call Alice and tell her we were on our way, but it somehow got lost in the shuffle. I grilled him carefully on the parts I thought unclear. What were they serving in the school cafeteria that day? What Degas painting did he see at the Featherstone Academy? Why would anyone want to summon Asmodeus, as opposed to say Demogorgon, who wears, after all, two hats?

Not that Myron did all the talking! I had a lot to teach him. There was so much he didn't know. He'd never seen the ruins of Mu or beautiful Kandam. He was only dimly aware of the peregrinations of the planet Proserpine. He wanted to hear all about the wide world he'd only brushed the surface of. He wanted to hear about the ambitions of Evelyn, the elephant, and the vast wanderings of Svipdag, the wolverine. But most of all, he wanted to hear about me, your humble narrator.

And so: My name is not Arthur Hong, although I own, or have owned, a birth certificate that claims it is. The date, re-inked so many times, started to seep through the paper, and I haven't had recourse to it in a while. My earliest memories are of the jungle, of trees laden with fruit, of unknown dangers on the forest floor but relative safety deep in the branches. I learned eventually, painfully, that leopards could kill my brothers and sisters, but they could not kill me.

How long this went on for, I do not know—I could not

count, nor speak, nor did these ideas mean anything to me. It was when I met humans, and found I could assume their form, that I first began to understand the concept of understanding. The first humans I met tried to burn me, assuming I was a demon, but I just laughed until the fire burned away the ropes that bound me, and then I showed them what a bearcat is made of. The battered remnant tried to make me their god, but I preferred to return to the binturongs. In this way, coming back and forth between the trees and the villages, I saw generations of humans spring up and die, I saw whole people, unique tribes with unique methods of face painting and dress, rise up and disappear. The Khoanh massacred and replaced the Naga who had massacred and replaced the stegosaurus-riding, snake-worshiping Lodidapurans who had massacred and replaced the first peoples I knew. I wasn't lying about the endless genocide. History is one long more- or less-successful genocide. But, really (I would like to ask any human I meet), what difference does it make if your people are done in by violence or not? They will, in time, forget all that made them your people. They will turn to strange customs and strange gods. Your grandchildren's grandchildren will be unrecognizable to you, why do you weep if they are murdered? They've already murdered your people by forgetting their ways. We pretend that life among the inhabitants of prehistory had an ancient continuity, but I saw what happened, and I can assure you that was not true. Their memories were short. An antediluvian custom to them was one that was eighty years old. After two generations, when I appeared again among them, they had no memory of me. Often their language had changed beyond recognition.

The number of people arriving and dying seemed to me infinite and arbitrary. I did not realize for quite some time that the invaders had had to come from somewhere. And once I realized that, I had to find out where they came from. I traveled from tree to tree to the edge of the jungle, and there I came across a body of water broader than the Mekong in flood. I assumed it was infinite, but men in boats came over it, from distant islands. I tried to swim in the water, which was salty and foul, but was always thrown back on shore, half drowned.

The people around me, meanwhile, had started getting better at doing things. They could make buildings out of stones instead of sticks, now, but this innovation was not quite enough to impress me. I traveled north, and when I reached the outposts of China I realized that people did not spring up autochthonous like ants. I began to have an idea of the world, an inaccurate, skewed idea of the world, but an idea nonetheless. For the first time I learned to speak a language with a sense of time, of long periods of time. For the first time I realized how much time had passed.

There followed an infinitude of adventures and imprisonments and condemnations and hairsbreadth escapes.

I would like to draw a character sketch of me. But the

truth is that most people's characters can be identified best negatively, by the things they haven't done. And there is very little I haven't done. I have never flown an airplane without crashing it, I guess, but little else. The modern age, temporarily and psychotically, values experience above all else, and my life would sound appealing to moderns, but they forget how many bad things there are to do. Murder, slaving, probably genocide—if you waited around long enough, you'd end up doing them, too. There is very little anyone can avoid doing forever, there are only things you can put off until you die. Sure, I've gone a hundred years without killing anyone. I can do a hundred years in my sleep. But try doing a thousand. That's the difference, proportionally, between going without water for one day and going without water for ten days. I know which one a human could do.

Vampires, it is true, do horrible things, but this is not because they are undead. It is because they have forever.

Ahashverosh, called by some the Eternal Jew, was a good friend of mine in the twelfth century, when he wandered over to the courts of the Angkor kings, and he had kept kosher for all those years of his existence; I ran into him in a Wendy's ten years ago, and he was eating a cheeseburger. Sheepishly he shrugged at me. He made almost two millennia without going astray, but the thought of a looming third was too much for him. And frankly, he had it easy: his rules hadn't changed out from underneath him. For anyone else, all virtue turns to vice once someone else comes along and redefines things. There have been times when massacring a whole bunch of children seemed not just like a tempting idea, but like the right decision, and everyone patted you on the back for it, and two hundred years later everyone who patted you on the back is dead, and suddenly they decide you're a monster. Torquemada of the Spanish Inquisition was a hero before he became a watchword for cruelty. Attila never got anything but approval from the other Huns for any slaughter he perpetrated. They were good men first, and only later did flighty people change their minds.

At this thought, some turn up their nose and insist that massacres have always been evil, and will always be evil, and they refuse to consider the way mores change. But these people, too, will die, and so will their belief, and their future will look back at them aghast, picking through their lives and finding something they did to be horrified by. And then massacres will come back into vogue. They always do.

Spenser is one, or was one, who tended to get up on a high horse about massacres and murders, as though everyone in the past was supposed to guess that the early twenty-first century would find them distasteful. It's bully for him that the world temporarily came around to his point of view, but he's like a man who has always worn skinny ties, elated that fashion has started requiring what he has in his wardrobe already. "At last they've figured it out!" he crows, unaware that in a year or two he will appear hopelessly out of date, as fashion travels on, leaving him floundering in its wake. Deep down, Spenser was too much of an optimist, a romantic—in a word, he still believed in stuff, and it is for this reason that he was constantly disappointed.

Alice, incidentally, disagrees with most of the above.

Once you figure out what's going on, and once you remove the possibility of being a good or bad individual, life becomes a series of meaningless incidents. There is the tedium of pretending to acquaintances that you grow older; there is the necessity of establishing new identities. The Everblums (see below) found this delightfully novel, but they've only done it once. Nothing will you ever do only once. Yawning on the latest roller coaster, yawning on the latest hoverbike, yawning through the latest planetarium or cinema show, you sleepwalk forward through history.

I bought many years ago and have inherited from myself time and again a modest brownstone in Boston. My needs are slight. I enjoy fruit juices and a warm fire. I would have gone mad long since if I didn't have the justification of my art.

The sketches of that whimsical parodist Plentygood van Dutchhook brought me a small measure of renown in 1811. I was rather slavishly aping Washington Irving, but I found it a simple matter to adopt a different pseudonym when I had evolved a different style. And briefly I wrote, as promised, pellucidly. Through two centuries that style declined. It is difficult, when you are sleepwalking through history, not to sleepwalk through prose as well. Scenes and characters repeated themselves in my books, because after a while, in life, scenes and characters repeat themselves—but when you're writing under six or seven names, this can look like a case of plagiarism. Clichés lose their ability to horrify because novelty itself seems so tired now. Aren't all the most important things that could be said clichés? I love you. I beg of you. Prepare to die. Anything truly beautiful became commonplace long ago, and now we sneer at it. But you start thinking this way and all you can write are adventure series or (on rare occasions) Maoist propaganda tracts. And now *The Magic Pony Club*.

Oh, but Myron, Myron! Stop me! This is your story, after all, it's all your story! You're the first new thing under the sun I have to write about in so long. I should be talking about you!

2.

We stayed two days in that flea trap. We talked about literature, the secret history, all the things that Myron had seen. There was so much to teach him. Even the simple things everyone else already knew—that it was easier to murder one of us than a human, because humans left behind a body, while we just turned into an animal corpse, and who paid attention to those?; that mixing candy corns and cheese crackers made a tasty snack; that we, as immortals, were completely sterile—he knew none of it. And he was in seventh heaven, being cooped up in a room with his hero. His hero, a typewriter, and room service. I would be surprised if he ever had a better time in his life—in his life that he could remember, I mean.

It was only two days, but in my memory it stretches out to weeks. In my memory I pretend we had no car, and we walked across the western states, sleeping under the stars.

All those two days I kept taking notes about Myron and his odyssey. We could have stayed longer—I could have extracted from Myron all those colorful little details that lend a degree of verisimilitude to a narrative—except that after a complimentary continental breakfast we went for a stroll around the bleak and arid grounds. There in the chill air, reclining near an empty pool, was a dark-haired woman in a lime bikini. I didn't recognize her with the sunglasses and the dye job, but she said hello, and I knew we were doomed.

I tipped my hat politely and hurried Myron away. He wanted to know who it was, of course.

"That was the Baroness von Everblum, and it's not her I'm worried about—it's her husband and twin brother."

"What? Ew!"

We had hustled into the lobby and were headed back to our room. "The Baron von Everblum is the worst gossip I've ever met. He also can't stop talking about how the two of them found the nagbu-thorn, and how it grants them eternal youth, which is really annoying. They're thirty-five and they look twenty-seven, big deal—it's just not that impressive!"

"Are they alchemists?"

"No, they're no one, they're just in the scene."

And just as we turned a corner, there was the baron, dressed in plaid shorts and a pink polo shirt. His hair was also dyed, bright flaming red.

"Why, Arthur! Fancy meeting you here. It has been an age of dogs. You are looking young, of course. You will notice that I, too, have not aged, thank you to the nagbu-thorn of Utnapishtim, Lord of the Source of Streams."

"Yes, yes. Good to see you. The baroness is by the pool, did you know that?"

He was not so easily ditched. "You'll note that we are both in disguise. It would be awkward if we ran into old acquaintances who recognized us and wanted to know our secret, the secret of the nagbu-thorn."

I was trying to hide Myron behind me, but he couldn't help peeking out.

"Why, what is this?" cried the baron. "This must be the young man the Brotherhood of Moloch was raving about."

Myron, God bless him, lacks the ability to blend in anywhere except a trauma ward.

"You were supposed to speak at a conference, no? Where are you going now? Speak up, young man. You look so startled, your mouth is like my blood, for it is *a positive O*." He laughed hysterically.

"Nowhere," Myron said.

"We really should go, your lordship," I said, doling the honorific out as a lagniappe to flatter him, but refusing to go so far as to give it a capital letter. Perhaps, therefore, it was not good enough for him, and he kept talking.

"You're heading west, aren't you? You must be, for you have come from the Michigan states. And you are dressed so warmly. It must not be to the Southwest you are going, for it is warm there."

Myron hummed nervously.

"San Francisco, perhaps? But no, your eyes betray you; it is not San Francisco. Seattle? Portland? Ah, Portland! Arthur, you should tell your charge not to be so obvious. His mouth does not twitch, perhaps due to nerve damage, but in his eyes, his naked desire for Portland is so evident."

"Fine," I said, "you got us, you're a caution, Baron. Now come on, kid, let's get started. It's a long drive."

The baron said, as we left, "Gang aft eagle." He was laughing uproariously again.

"What does that mean?" Myron asked as we locked ourselves in our room.

I was packing up the typewriter. "It means the best laid plans don't always work out. Also, he's an idiot." I was so distracted as we headed for the car that I accidentally paid the hotel bill.

3.

Myron couldn't make a journey without imagining himself a Jules Verne character, so he was distracted with all of that, but me, I was worried. It was a straight shot along

I-80 W from Chicago through Grand Island to Sacramento, and it wouldn't take much skill with a map and a ruler to extrapolate our actual destination. On the other hand, veering north was out of the question: the baron was already on his ham radio telling everyone we were aiming for Portland. But veering south was also out of the question, as any fool who knew that we knew the baron knew we were supposed to head north would assume we would head south in reaction. Probably the smartest thing to do would be to turn back, but I didn't want to run into the Everblums again. Just to be safe, first chance I had I stopped at a post office and mailed all my notes to my Boston PO box.

Myron apologized for giving away his secret, but I told him not to worry about it. He was just too honest, was all.

I went fast—everyone goes fast on this highway, there's nothing to slow down for—and I would have gone faster except the Bug was pretty old. We hit Salt Lake City at nightfall, and I kept on driving. It was dawn, an hour outside of Reno, when a bat came down and buzzed the windshield. I knew what such auspices augured, so I pulled over. The bat wheeled around and landed next to the car and became a scrawny, naked, middle-aged man with a face like a leather mask. I rolled down the window. It was Allambee.

"I've got a message from Angel, mate. It's about the car," Allambee said. He always started any dialogue with a *mate* or two, to remind you he was Australian.

"Tell him if it was a gift, I thank him for it; and if it was a loaner, I'm not done with it yet," I said.

"He wants it back. I don't think he's cranky, mate, he just wants it back. He said to drive it to Campanile, and he'll meet you there, probably tomorrow."

"Where's Campanile again?" I asked, although I knew perfectly well. It was a few miles north, past the reservoir, along a road we'd already passed—just where Allambee said it was. "He'll be there tomorrow, then?" I asked. "No need for me to go right away?"

"Nah, mate. You might catch some drama if you go on, though. There's a whole fleet of bullymen up ahead."

"What's a bullyman?" Myron asked. Allambee ignored him.

"He means there're a lot of cops up ahead," I explained. "Maybe I'll go right to Campanile now. I don't know where the registration for this heap is, and I wouldn't want anything to get impounded," I said, "before I can deliver the car in Campanile."

Allambee just shrugged. "No worries," he said. "Mate." And then he was flying away.

"Are the cops after us?" Myron asked when he was gone.

"It's plausible," I said. I'd cut a few corners in my life.

"And is this guy really going to meet you in Campanile?"

"It's plausible," I said.

"So you think it's safe?"

"No, I think it's a trap, but it's a plausible one."

"I think it's a trap, too," Myron said. "He never even looked at me. Everyone always looks at me." *Before,* he didn't add, looking away.

I was testing the wind with my hand, and it was blowing strong, maybe even strong enough to cover our tracks behind us. "I think it's a trap," I said, "because I always think it's a trap. But here's the plan. We'll go off the road and drive across the desert, along the reservoir spillway. This has the advantage of being the most direct route to Campanile, in case there's a bat watching us start off. I doubt if he'll follow us far, though, he must be tired out from flying around all night looking for us. After we get to the reservoir, we drive the car right in. Then we spend the next three or four days underwater, breathing through this cardboard tube, until the whole thing gets called off. Then we walk to Campanile and get something to eat. It's the last place they'd expect us to be."

"There's only one tube," Myron said.

I gunned the engine. "We'll take turns," I said. I realize what I was proposing sounded crazy, but I'd gotten out of many a scrape before by simply waiting someplace extremely uncomfortable, like a refrigerator or the bottom of an outhouse, until everyone else got bored with looking. The worse the place was, the less likely anyone would think you could spend any time, let alone the month I spent under the outhouse, there. "Anyway, it's not like we can actually drown."

This was my plan, and it turned out to be a terrible one. Driving across the desert I had to roll up all the windows, because the wind was kicking dust and sand into the car, and with the windows up—there was no air conditioning—the car became unbearably stifling.

"Is that the reservoir?" Myron asked, looking out his window. "There's no water in it."

"That's just some kind of secondary reservoir. If the first one fills up, they can send the runoff down the spillway, and it fills up this one. Don't worry, there'll be plenty of water when we get there."

"I was hoping it would be dry," pouted Myron, but I ignored him. I eased over now to drive along the edge of the spillway, along the concrete lip where our tracks were hardest to see in the thin spray of shifting sand. We were only a couple hundred yards from the reservoir and our aquatic adventure, and the ground was sloping upward gently, when suddenly my nose twitched, and something behind a bush up ahead, in the shadow of the bush, something that I had thought was a rock, turned out to be a man hiding under a gray duster. He threw the duster off and took a step and turned into an enormous bison, which charged forward. I stepped on the gas, but the car, the car was not so fast, and its wheels were still spinning for traction in the dusting of sand when two thousand pounds of bison crashed inexorably into the side of the car, right behind my seat. We skidded sideways over the steep edge of the spillway, which was, of course, dry, so our tumble down was very painful. I dragged myself painfully and a little bloodily out the shattered driver's side window of the upside-down car, reached in for my duffle bag, and then helped Myron crawl across and avoid the glass. He was still holding his duffle bag, its cloth handle gripped tightly and probably unconsciously in one hand.

The spillway was festooned with foot-high concrete cones sticking up from the ground. As I understand it, water coming into the spillway from the reservoir would hit the cones, which was supposed to dissipate the kinetic energy of the flood. The spillway was only fifteen feet deep, but the car, after flipping over, had landed on the field of concrete cones, and they had punched right through the roof, battering the two of us. Myron had gotten it worse; he was bleeding rather badly from his head and wasn't making much sense.

"Kid, we've got to get going," I said. I pulled him over to the far side of the spillway, his duffle bag dragging behind him, to where there was a metal ladder in a shallow recess. But when I grabbed the lowest rung the whole ladder came free and fell over backwards, breaking apart into three pieces on the ground. The trap was a good one. I looked around quickly: there were other ladders every fifty feet or so, but they were probably also rigged. As a binturong I could climb the walls, of course—binturongs can climb anything red pandas can climb, and red pandas can climb anything—but there was no way to bring Myron with me. Our only hope,

I figured, was to head toward the reservoir and climb the stepped embankment to the release gate; we should be able to clamber out from there. It was when I turned in that direction that I saw her. Ten feet away. The rising sun was striking her left side, casting deep shadows across half her face. She was wearing a white cotton dress, and even at the bottom of the spillway there was enough wind to billow it out and blow her short hair back and forth in her face. It was Mignon Emanuel.

"Myron," I whispered, suddenly thinking of something I wished I had thought of days ago. "This tube hasn't left your sight since you got it, right? No one could have pulled a switcheroo on us, right?"

But Myron was too dazed to say anything coherent. He kept babbling and making horrible groaning sounds. Then Mignon Emanuel spoke.

"Myron. Arthur," she said, with a nod for each.

It was disconcerting, even after hearing what Myron had told me about her abilities, to be in the presence of a therianthrope and feel nothing, no comforting or warning tingle. It was like she wasn't there at all. "Angel's expecting us," I told her, just in case that would do some good.

At Mignon Emanuel's side was a purse, and she reached in and removed a furry severed head.

"Is that a dog?" Myron asked at last, shaking his head.

"It's a coyote," I said. "It's Angel Sanchez."

"Angel Sanchez is a coyote?" Myron asked. Like I said, he'd hurt his head and wasn't thinking straight.

"Is the lion here?" I asked. I admit I was terrified.

"No. Benson has left his employ and is assisting me now."

I let out a sigh of relief. Lynch was the one I was really worried about.

"I would first like to say that I'm sorry all this was necessary," Mignon Emanuel said. "I hope you understand that I bear you no personal animosity, Arthur."

"Bear?" Myron said, suddenly remembering where he was. "Watch out, she can turn into a bear." The blood was flowing so freely from his head that it completely covered one eye. It got into his mouth as he talked, and he had to spit it out.

"I know," I said.

"And, Myron, I do apologize that it has come to this."

"Are you going to kill us?" Myron asked.

"What? Why, of course not, Myron. I'm here to help you, just as I always have been. I make no claims to altruism, although I am personally fond of you. You understand that I am in need of you, just as I flatter myself that you are in need of me." She took a step forward.

"You killed Spenser!" Myron shouted at her.

"Spenser and I had a feud of long standing. That had little to do with you, Myron. There are things you don't know about *Alces alces,* the moose. You would not blame me if you knew all I knew."

"He's the only person I've met in the last six months who didn't just lie to me all the time!" Myron was crying now. He was so upset that he forgot to add what he had clearly meant to, which was *except for Arthur* or *present company excluded*.

"Myron, I only lied to you for your own good. I need you to help me to bring an end to all this violence. We spoke before of unifying our people. We can unify them under your banner. Even if we know you're not the chosen one, no one else knows that."

"Why can't you leave me alone? Why can't all of you leave me alone?"

Up ahead I could see someone naked, probably Benson, standing up at the reservoir. Doubtless, if anything went wrong here, he could open the floodgates and fill the spillway with a wall of water. Anyone in the path of the flood would be pulped. It wouldn't kill us, of course, but it would be easy for Benson to follow the spillway down to the second reservoir and fish the bodies out to finish us off. A thirty-pound binturong stands little chance against a bear, but Benson's hand on the trigger made sure even any mismatched combat that took place wouldn't be a fair fight.

Mignon Emanuel, meanwhile, said, "You're too special to be left alone." She took another step forward and held out her hand, bending forward at the waist. "Your friend Arthur can leave, no harm will come to him."

Myron was sniffling beside me. I liked the sound of some of this, but just to be safe, I had reached into my duffle bag. Assuming no one had pulled a switcheroo—assuming the maneuver I had practiced years ago I was still proficient at—I had pried off the cap at one end of the tube, and I could feel the wadded-up tinfoil inside.

"I'm not the only one who needs you, Myron," Mignon Emanuel said. "Don't let us all down."

"I don't believe you anymore," Myron screamed, and punched her in the face.

For a moment we all stood frozen. It was not a very good punch—Myron would never have strong arms, and he didn't really know what he was doing—but he did catch Mignon Emanuel completely by surprise. Finally, very slowly and deliberately, Mignon Emanuel said, "No one in a thousand years has struck me with impunity. I hope you will take it as a token of my esteem that I am willing to forget this has happened."

"I hate you," Myron screamed, and punched her again, more confidently this time, and right in the nose, from which descended a trickle of red.

Mignon Emanuel's face darkened into something truly terrifying. Rearing up, she roared, "If you have drawn blood, the binturong will die."

At that moment my senses became clouded—or, better, overwhelmed. I was ready for it, of course, or thought I was, but it was still a bit of a surprise, the powerful emanation from the tube. It was the emanation of death, the stench emitted from the bones of an immortal when his life has fled. I had counted on this stench, when the time came, paralyzing my opponent, but Myron and Mignon Emanuel both turned their heads immediately toward me as, in a great rustling of tinfoil, I drew out of the tube the bones of a tiger's forearm and front paw, bleached a beautiful white and bound together with silver wire. If Mignon Emanuel, still drawn up to her full height, paused a moment there, it was not from terror or surprise at the miasma that filled the spillway; it was rather from the paralysis that accompanies a sudden realization. What she had realized just then I do not pretend to know.

And the bones were moving. Theoretically, when I had practiced this maneuver, the strike came smoothly as I drew the skeletal arm from the tube, like a samurai's quick-draw *iaijutsu* strike, but the tube had been shaken around so much, things had shifted around inside, and I bobbled the draw, and even dropped the tube. But I was committed, and I swung the bones forward, holding the elbow like a club.

Mignon Emanuel murmured, out loud, "So that's where that went," just as the five claws struck her throat. Very few things are sharper than a tiger's claws, and Mignon Emanuel's neck exploded in a spray of red. Her face darkened again, just before it blanched, and I worried for a moment that she would be able to turn into a bear before she died—bears, as everyone knows, can keep fighting and killing even after they die. But her eyes rolled back, and she flopped over onto the cement ground. In death, as we always do, she assumed her true form, and her clothing exploded into scraps. From a distance, the wind brought me the sound of Benson's startled cry.

"Listen, kid, we're in real danger, he's going to open the

floodgates," I said rapidly as I knelt by her corpse and set to work. Suddenly a battery of sirens began to sound, making it even harder to think. With the razor-sharp claws of the immortal tiger I made a cut down the bear's belly, from sternum to navel. The guts exploded outward in a disgusting mass, and I began shoveling them away.

Myron was still standing there, sniffling.

I had to shout. "If we get swept downstream, Benson will find us at the end, battered and torn, and finish us off." I paused a moment. Benson might not be smart enough to search the secondary reservoir, but he was probably under orders from Mignon Emanuel, and he'd be able to follow orders. Also, Florence could be down there right now, ready to dive in the water and eviscerate the bloody remains of our bodies before we could even regain consciousness. The siren's wailing could not cover up the great mechanical whirring up ahead. I unspooled the bear's intestines faster.

"Kid, listen, you've got to get inside," I said at last.

"What? No!"

"Fifty billion tons of water" — (I may have been exaggerating) — "are about to come down this chute. The insides of this bear are the only soft thing for miles."

I grabbed him by the shoulders and began to muscle him toward the bear's corpse. It would have been difficult to actually force him in, but fortunately he relented and stuck his feet into the guts. At my instigation, he positioned himself so he was oriented in the opposite direction as the bear, his feet toward its head, and nestled himself lower and lower, slithering in backwards with his feet up inside the rib cage, until he was up to his shoulders in guts. He had somehow managed to wedge his duffle bag in there, too. The big holdup for him was getting his hands in—for some reason he didn't want to do that part—but eventually he wriggled those in, too. I noticed that his head had stopped bleeding, but, of course, he now was almost completely covered in gore. I thought for a moment of turning back into a binturong and trying to worm in next to him, but, on careful consideration, I realized there would not be enough space, not with his bag in there, too, and there was no time to draw it back out.

"This is important," I shouted at him, over the sirens and the clanking of chains, and—was that the rushing of water? "When your wild ride stops, you will still be in danger. Swim out as soon as you can, and run to the road. The road is south, you know which way is south?"

"The sun is on my left," he said. The image must have reminded him of the terror of Mignon Emanuel standing in the rising sun five minutes ago, and he choked a little on the answer.

"Good. Don't get caught, but if you get caught blame everything on me. I'll wait for you in Reno for three days, and then I'll head for Sacramento."

"But how—" Myron started. Clearly he was worried about me.

I cut him off. "In the Del Paso Heights branch of the

Sacramento Public Library, there's a book on the care and feeding of binturongs. Inside that book, there's an address—"

Some look in Myron's eyes stopped me. "Why?" Myron asked, squirming in his mattress of blood. "Why are you doing this for me?"

I thought of Myron's backpack, left in the back of Alice's pickup truck so many months ago. "Because you liked my books," I said. Because how could I tell him the real answer, that I envied the hell out of him? He was young—I don't mean he was literally young, he was thousands of years old, just like the rest of us—but he was young because he had no past to haunt him. He didn't have hundreds of murders on his conscience, he didn't have the stupefying dullness of having seen and done everything already, so that even the promises offered by the new technologies of the future—faster cars and 3-D television—seemed like tedious variations on a tired theme. Envy was why the lion wanted to kill him, envy was why the bear wanted to use him. The memories of an endless childhood among the jungles, or the wastelands, or the savannahs, an endless childhood that finally ended, haunted us the way nostalgia haunts an old man, but our nostalgia cannot be ended by senility and a natural death. To see someone who returned, thanks to a lion's claws passing through his brain, to the garden of that childhood—there was nothing more heartening and heartbreaking.

But there was no way to say all this. By now the roar of water was deafening. I picked up all the intestines I could in one armload and jammed them on top of Myron's face, forcing his head down as deep into bear bowels as I could. "Watch out for the lion, the one to fear is the lion," I shouted, perhaps futilely. Then the water was all around, and I had to leap for the side. Halfway through the leap, I turned into a binturong, and, my mass now a quarter of what it had been when I jumped, I was able to grab the side, and, my claws finding purchase in the small cracks, to scamper up it. My shaggy prehensile tail got wet.

The last thing I noticed about Myron's makeshift escape pod, as it raced down the river, was that in death Mignon Emanuel reclaimed the aura she had lost in life. I could feel the presence of her corpse behind me as it sailed downstream, and out of range.

X

The West Coast

The man who will wantonly kill a poor brute for sport will think little of murdering a fellow-creature. Now, boys, we have but one chance left—the Diamond Cave.

R. M. Ballantyne, *The Coral Island*

I.

I will never really be certain of what happened next. I didn't see Myron again, and although Alice did, it was only for a short while, and she didn't get the details. Certainly he escaped. I escaped, too, and my pursuit across the desert by Benson (which included a thrilling scene of two naked men climbing the reservoir's control station and more than three carjackings) was harrowing enough to fill a chapter of its own. Let us assume Myron's was equally exciting.

His next actions can only be pieced together in retrospect, and after much research. He had no money, nothing but the meager contents of his duffle bag. He was covered in the guts of a bear. He looked like Myron. Everything was against him.

It appears from eyewitness accounts that he probably worked in a carnival in or around Medford, Oregon. He had almost certainly read *Toby Tyler: or, Ten Weeks with a Circus*, and the idea doubtless appealed to him. But how he found his way to Oregon in the first place is more speculative. There were sightings at a cockfight in Redding, California, and at a UFO convention in Susanville. Several witnesses insisted they saw Myron collecting tickets at a wax museum in Lovelock, Nevada, which is frankly pretty far out of his way, and their testimony may be discounted by the incredulous.

However he got there, it was almost May before Myron reached Portland. He came in on foot, with the sun rising directly behind him. His clothes were tattered; a huge backpack was on his back. A scarf draped loosely around his face concealed his features. The town was just waking up. Myron climbed the stairs to the Broadway Bridge, its passenger walkway separated from the whizzing cars by a low metal fence. Portland is the crown jewel in the kingdom of vagabonds, and by vagabonds I mean nothing more romantic than homeless drug addicts and the mentally ill. On the bridge, Myron was just one itinerant among many, for here several dozen had decided to spend the night. Each of them had a huge backpack, and they were sleepily getting up to face the day. And then, as Myron watched, they began to jump up and run, run toward him. He was jostled back and forth by the crowd until he got thrown against the railing, and, gazing through the bars down at the Willamette River below, he held his place in relative comfort while the human tide passed. And when they had passed, and he looked ahead on the bridge, he saw what everyone had been running from. There was an Indian man, his rags and his enormous backpack no different from anyone else's, except that he had in his hands a bow. A quiver of arrows was attached to his belt, the cap off and dangling from a string. One arrow he had already nocked, and it glowed with an eerie bluish light. It was not one of the Nine Unknown Men, but it was an employee of the Nine Unknown Men, and he knew just enough of things to be dangerous. Dantaghata.

The only witnesses to the following events, except for Myron and his nemesis, were those few beggars who had huffed too much paint the night before to be able to stand this morning. These are not the most creditable of witnesses, and yet by triangulating their stories we may be able to reach something close to a true account of the events of that morning. Surely it is plausible that at the moment Myron sighed and said, "Look. Look. I'm sorry I beat you."

"You didn't beat me, *moron*," the Indian man spat out. "You beat my brother."

"Your bother?"

"My twin brother. Did you think I was chasing you across the country just because I lost some silly game to you? You really are stupid."

"Your twin brother?" Myron said. "You mean you're not Dantaghata?"

"Of course I'm Dantaghata, you nitwit. Who else could I be? My brother died in the West Village, gunned down thanks to your monkeyshines."

Myron was beginning to get a little flustered from the constant stream of insults. "You're after me because you think I killed your brother? I didn't even kill him."

"Try to listen to what I say, you ugly retard," Dantaghata said. "I didn't say you killed him, just that you caused him to die. You lured him to his death, and so it's your fault."

"I didn't even know he was dead! Why aren't you going after the Illuminati?"

"You must think I'm crazy. Attack the Illuminati? Are you trying to kill me? They're the *Illuminati!*"

"They were at the conference you busted up. Why didn't you go after them then?"

For a moment Dantaghata's face became a mask of absolute terror. "They were there?" he managed to stammer out. But he shrugged it off. "That's all in the past. I've tracked you from coast to coast, and I've brought with me the Pashupatastra." He flexed his bow, and the arrow's blue light flared and dimmed. "When this arrow strikes, it unmakes not only this universe, but also the next two universes to be created in the future. Lord Rama disdained to use it, but I am not about to be talked out of things as easily, you stain."

Myron looked to his right and left for an avenue of escape. The fence along both sides would not have been much of an obstacle to anyone, say, five feet tall. The only way Myron could go was straight back, which didn't seem like a good idea.

"I really don't want to die," Myron said.

"Boo hoo hoo. We don't always get what we want."

"Are you sure it's a good idea to unmake the whole universe just to get me?"

"Am I sure? Are you kidding? Of course I'm sure!"

Myron probably looked sad at that moment.

"Any last words?" Dantaghata said, testing his pull one last time. "Before I kill you, I mean, loser."

"As a matter of fact . . ."

Witnesses were unable to report with any degree of accuracy, so greatly were they swooning just then, what Myron's words were, but I feel safe making the assumption that they were in the neighborhood of: "Pax sax sarax . . ."

Dantaghata fell sideways against the railings; then his legs gave way, and he hit the ground. His bow and arrow clattered around him, and his quiver spilled out as well, arrows everywhere. According to one witness, a teenage runaway with high hopes (as they all have) who had ended up six months later addicted to compressed air and half insane (as they all are) on the bridge—but who was fortuitously out of earshot—Myron ran forward immediately to grab the archer's weapons, but his foot, in his excitement, hit the bow, and it skidded under the railing and over the side of the bridge, to the river below. Myron went to pick up the blue glowing arrow, but none of them were blue and glowing at that moment, and whatever eldritch symbols had been carved in the wood Myron could not read, so as Dantaghata began to stir, he grabbed an arrow at random and ran ahead, past him some space. By the time Dantaghata had struggled to his feet, Myron had fished his own little battered compound bow from his backpack. The arrow, when he nocked it, was comically overlong for the tiny bow.

"What does this arrow do?" he shouted. "Does it unmake creation?"

Dantaghata had struggled to his feet again. He was sweating profusely (the witness reports), and looked horrified. But he was canny enough, his faculties had already returned.

"That's the suicide arrow," he said.

But the arrow, at nock, was changing and shifting. Its bronze tip became the head of a snake, which opened its mouth to display long, cruel fangs, and hissed.

This, witnesses agreed, was "trippy."

"It looks like some kind of snake arrow," Myron observed.

Dantaghata licked his lips. "The Nagastra. Its poison bite is certain death."

Myron nodded. That sounded about right.

Dantaghata said, "Put it down before you injure yourself, little boy."

Myron drew back the bow.

"You can't even hurt me," Dantaghata said. "I'm like a wheel made meticulously over a month by a craftsman who can make five chariots in a day."

Myron took careful aim.

"Like a drop of vinegar in a jug of milk, alone I can spoil whole armies."

"You done?" Myron asked.

"Very well," Dantaghata said. "As you killed my brother, so shall you kill me. Very well." And he began to cry.

"Stop it," Myron said.

Still sobbing. "The burning ground has seen the back of every man. No man has seen its back."

"Cut it out."

It is here that I wish I could have spoken to Myron. I would like to know what he was thinking, now that he had his enemy in his sights. Was he thinking about those years when he had had reason to believe that no one wanted to kill him? Was he reviewing the deaths he had seen recently, the violence and the fear that followed him like a hungry dog?

What was the thought process, I want to ask him, that led him to do something as stupid as what he did? "Ah, screw it," he said, and threw the arrow and bow over the side of the bridge to the river below. The snake head screamed all the way down. "Just leave me alone," he also said, and turned and walked away. He had gotten maybe thirty feet, when he heard that familiar grating voice behind him calling out.

"I had a second bow in my backpack, tardo."

Myron turned, and there, indeed, behind him, was Dantaghata, a bow, a slightly different bow, in his hands. The arrow he had drawn back glowed blue. Doubtless, Myron felt so tired.

"Goodbye, universe," Myron said.

"Shut up, megadouche," Dantaghata said.

And then he released the arrow.

What happened next there is perfect unanimity on. Dantaghata released the arrow, but the arrow did not move. The arrow stayed in one place, and the bow Dantaghata was holding moved backwards instead. It moved backwards as it straightened out, but then it continued to move backwards, and Dantaghata was moving forward at the same time. In fact, they were both shrinking, or contracting. The bow and Dantaghata's body moved closer and closer as the arm separating them shortened, and soon the arm was so short that the body and the bow overlapped, and then they crossed, and then they were no more. The arrow stopped glowing, and it clattered to the ground.

The glue sniffers on the bridge were so terrified by this vision that to a man they swore repentance—but were they sober when they swore?

But Myron, Myron just turned away and walked across the bridge.

2.

Myron walked through northwest Portland until he came to an address he had scribbled on a piece of paper, copied from a library's phone book weeks earlier. The paper was damp and creased, but the number was still legible, and he double-checked: 408. It was the Twenty-Four-Hour Church of Elvis. Next to it was a wooden door, which at first appeared to bear no sign, until Myron noticed the red-tinted window set in it. The glass was in the shape of a flower, quartered—the rose and the cross.

Off to one side an animal that resembled a large red cat, her fur impossibly soft and bright with white and black highlights, was pacing back and forth, waving her striped bushy tail and occasionally making a little jump. She seemed to be trying to catch Myron's eye. He studiously ignored her, although the back of his neck must have been tingling like crazy, and tested the door—it was unlocked.

The frisking animal darted forward as Myron entered the building, but the door shut in her face. It is therefore on no red panda's testimony that I base the following account. My source, though reliable, must remain anonymous, for the Rosicrucians are known above all else for being secretive. And unfortunately, I did not get from him all this information until much later.

Myron found, inside the door, a dark wooden staircase, going down, at the foot of which stood a tiny, three-foot-tall door with a wooden plaque. It read, in several alphabets and languages, among which Myron recognized Spanish, Hebrew, and something that was probably Chinese—and rather prim English, fortunately—WHOM ARE YOU HERE TO SEE? The bottom few steps were littered with cigarette butts, limp colonic nozzles, and broken glass.

"Um," Myron said. "The grandmaster of the Rosicrucians?"

The door clicked, then swung half-open, away from him.

Myron pushed it and ducked through—into the most sumptuously gaudy room he had ever seen. Every surface, walls, floor and ceiling, was covered with a glittering mosaic of mirrors. In the corners, fountains and waterfalls trickled water musically through a labyrinth of chimes. And at the far end, atop a dais, blossomed a multicolored throne, its armrests wide and curled, its back branching out like lily petals. And upon the throne sat a man clad head to foot in batik robes. He glowered in uncomfortable silence.

Myron stood there quietly, shifting awkwardly from foot to foot until he could take it no longer. "Excuse me," he said. "Are you the grandmaster of the Rosicrucians?"

"Fool!" roared the man on the throne. "I am but the slave of his slave!" And leaping to his feet, he gestured with a sweep of his arm toward the wall. Myron's eyes, adjusting to the chaos and the glistening, could just make out a small door, only three feet high, concealed amid the mosaic. Without another word, he went to it and ducked through.

The room on the far side was even more amazing than the one he had left. Every inch of the walls was gold—huge rectangular panels of gold, framed by golden borders traced with ornate helices of lapis lazuli. The floor was gold, and too precious to step on, so inch-high pedestals of red marble wound like stepping stones around the room.

Dozens of golden candelabras of varying heights festooned the room, and the combined strength of their candles, reflected off the golden walls and lit some parts of the room like midday, while leaving in corners and crevices deep shadows. Against one golden wall, atop twelve golden steps, rose a golden throne, with precious stones, jacinth and fire opal and purple amethyst, spelling out strange letters along its back. There, in golden robes, sat a scowling woman, her dark hair braided around a golden crown. She held a golden scepter topped with an enormous orb of black opal.

"I don't suppose," Myron said hesitantly, "that you're the grandmaster of the Rosicrucians?"

"Fool!" she shrieked. "I am but his slave!" She, too, leapt to her feet, her robes billowing around her, and several candles spontaneously extinguished. With the scepter she gestured toward a shadowy corner. Myron stepped uncertainly from marble stepstone to marble stepstone, reached the corner, and felt in the shadows another tiny doorway behind some drapery. It took him some time to rustle the drapery aside and duck through.

And there before him was a small garden. Light, blinding at first, streamed through a glass roof, playing off the flowering plants, rosebushes of various colors hovering over patches of daffodils and black-eyed Susans. Ferns peeped up in between the flowers. In a clearing a man wearing khaki shorts and a plain black T-shirt sat cross-legged on the mossy ground. Arrayed on the ground in front of him were a pair of wavy daggers fashioned together to make pruning shears, a set of jeweler's scales, and a paperback copy of *Sweet and Dismal: The Economics of Boxing*.

"Why are all the doorways so small?" Myron asked.

The man was staring off into space. "To teach humility to the supplicants who come, who must crawl through each door on their bellies, as we, incidentally, must to reach these same rooms ourselves. You alone have succeeded in thwarting our system. Congratulations! But this is hardly the question you came all this way to ask."

"Are you the grandmaster of the Rosicrucians?"

"I am, but this is not the question you want to ask, either."

"Oh, you're right," Myron said. "I guess what I want to ask is, what should I do? Who am I? How can I avoid being killed?"

"If you could boil that down to one question," the grandmaster said, still staring at something behind Myron, "what would it be?"

"Who am I?" Myron said. He was in the uncomfortable position of making a statement that was a question, but being so uncertain that he asked the statement like a question.

The grandmaster said, "You have asked the question that all people ask, sooner or later. However, I'm going to give you an answer slightly different from the answer I'd give another. As all three of your questions are really the same question, the answer to all three will be revealed on June twenty-seventh of this year, at approximately eight a.m., on San Clemente Island. Do you know where that is?"

"No."

"It's sixty-five miles west of San Diego. On the east side of this island, about south of the midway point of its length, you'll find a crude shack painted red. Not inside, but outside that shack, everything will be made clear."

"Everything will be made clear outside this shack?"

"On June twenty-seventh, at approximately eight in the morning."

"Where again?"

"South of halfway up the east coast of San Clemente Island, sixty-five miles west of San Diego."

Myron made a mental note of the details. Then he asked, "How do you know this?"

"I have an atlas."

"No, sorry, I mean," Myron said, "how do you know all will be revealed?"

"We have the Mason word and second sight. Things for to come we can foretell aright," the grandmaster said.

"And this is not a trap?" Myron said.

"It is not. But you should go alone."

Myron shifted uncomfortably from one foot to the other.

"If you would like to go, you might find it simpler to take the back way," the grandmaster said. He indicated a small door behind a rosebush.

"It's not that," Myron said. "It's just that it took me a long time to get here."

The grandmaster nodded.

"Well, I guess I'd expected something else. There was a lot of buildup."

The grandmaster was still gazing off at a point somewhere behind Myron. "Everything hidden will be revealed," he repeated. And what more could Myron ask for? The back door was behind the rosebush, and Myron went over to take it. As he was about to go out, he looked behind him and saw what the grandmaster was looking at. Mounted on the wall behind the door Myron had entered through was a flatscreen TV, and a Woody Woodpecker cartoon.

3.

The red panda waited for Myron out front, but he took the back way out, so we lost him again.

And he spent another few weeks off on his own. Spenser had taught him how to survive in the woods and Gloria had taught him how to survive in the city, while I had taught him, I would like to think, how to survive, period. It was no wonder no one could locate him.

But word trickled through the underground stream, as it always does. Arcane whispers of San Diego, and San Clemente Island. And so, late one June night unseasonably cold and cut through with a bitter wind, the red panda, prowling a marina north of San Diego, saw Myron casting the rope off a tiny launch no bigger than a rowboat. She sped down the dock and made a great leap, forepaws stretched out, bushy tail trailing behind her, and landed flat in the launch as Myron pushed it adrift with an oar.

Myron ignored the creature, so she turned into his old friend Alice.

"Jinkies, it's cold!" she cried.

Myron ignored her and awkwardly used the oar as a paddle to navigate his way out of the marina.

"How can it be so cold here, it's June?"

Myron, she noticed, had a strange look about him. Not his usual strange look—his eyes were glassy and preoccupied. He was sweating. He was wearing a yellow raincoat, and a heavy sweater underneath, which must have been warm.

"Myron, do you remember me? I'm Alice, we met last year in a pickup truck. I know Arthur."

Outside the shelter of the harbor, the wind really picked up. In the distance, flashes of lightning strobed in the sky.

"Myron, you should turn back—there's a storm coming. Actually, do you know what you're doing?" Ahead of them was nothing but the open sea.

"Kind of," Myron said.

"It is really cold out here," Alice said. "Do you have any spare clothes, a jacket or anything?"

"Nothing that would fit you," Myron said. So Alice turned back into a red panda, which is at least naturally furry.

As the California coast drifted farther away, Myron

checked a pocket compass and then moved to the back of the launch. There was a small motor there, and he fiddled with it for a long while before it started up. By this point the wind was blowing strong, and waves kept coming over the sides of the boat. The red panda tried to shake herself dry, like a dog. It got colder. But now that Myron, with the help of his compass, had oriented the boat properly, the wind was directly at their back and sped the little launch along.

Alice assumed the shape of a human and tried to warm herself in a life jacket. "Are we going to San Clemente Island?" she asked.

"If we're lucky," Myron said.

"You do know that's pretty far from shore?"

"Sixty-five miles. Or farther, I guess, because we'll have to round it to land."

"Are you sure this is a good idea, Myron?"

But Myron didn't answer that question, instead he said, "There's something I just barely can't remember, something like a dream from long ago, and it's on the tip of my tongue."

San Clemente lies diagonally and noodle-shaped in the Pacific, maybe twenty-five miles long but only a few miles wide. It contains a naval base and a unique subspecies of night lizard and very little else. Myron was aiming to round San Clemente on the south; if they went astray to the north, they'd probably hit the island, or one of the other Channel Islands. But if they went too far south, and passed the island without spotting it, the next possible landfall was Hawaii, and past that Australia. They wouldn't die, of course, but the weeks and months in an open boat with no drinking water would be in some ways worse than death.

Lightning illuminated the horizon again, and Alice pandaed and huddled beneath the seat. But then it got too wet down there, and she came back up, setting her paws on the edge of the boat and looking nervously at the sky. Myron kept his hand on the throttle, and his eye on the compass. They came upon a squall. The wind had just grown stronger and stronger, but it was almost always behind them, so they didn't notice so much until they saw that the rain ahead was falling almost horizontally. And then they were inside the rain, and Myron had to stop and bail, which slowed them down. By the time they motored clear, Myron's pants, which stuck out of the raincoat, were sopping, and Alice's fur was a soaking bedraggled mess. She had to go human again, and when she did she instantly regretted it.

And in her human times, did she ask Myron for the missing details of his adventures? Did she ask him what he was thinking during his exploits among the Rosicrucians, or how he slipped away from the Campanile reservoir? Or even where he got the boat or learned the proper approach to the island? No, she did not. What she said was, "Myron, I've got to warn you. Whatever Arthur told you, you mustn't listen to him. Don't listen to anything Arthur told you." I could have predicted that this is what she would have told him even if she had not later told me it was what she said.

"I feel strange," Myron said.

Thunder boomed, uncomfortably close.

Alice took her turn at the throttle while Myron bailed a little more. She considered turning the craft around, but she would never be able to make it all the way back in human form without coma-freezing, and, as a red panda Myron could easily wrest control from her thumbless paws and perhaps even dump her overboard.

"I feel strange," Myron said again. He was probably still sweating, despite the cold, although all the sea spray made it difficult to tell for certain. The smell of the sea was overpowering. Whatever it was he was having trouble remembering, he had not yet remembered. He hummed to himself.

It took several hours, but dawn had not yet broken when lights became visible high in the distance. These were the great cliffs of San Clemente, rising a quarter mile from the sea in some places.

"Wow," said Myron. "And the fisherman had said this was a suicide mission."

"A suicide mission?" Alice asked, assuming human form for that one anxious question.

"Going to sea in a boat this small. But it was okay after all. Now we just have to watch for the patrols."

The navy kept secrets on San Clemente Island, and it guarded these secrets jealously. Fishermen and divers were permitted to troll these waters, but no one may set foot on San Clemente, and watches and patrols enforced the stricture with a fanatical rigor. But today the lightning played about the top of San Clemente, and the wind, which had been blowing steadily for hours, was constantly threatening to whip the sea into a fury. So the sailors huddled safe in their secret underground bunkers. There was no one around.

The cliffs, when the launch reached them, were far too steep to scale, but Myron motored southeast to round the tip of the island. This brought them athwart the wind, and the launch was tossed and spun around almost helplessly. A freak wave rose up and dropped, to everyone's surprise, a broken and ragged net on top of them both. The red panda gnawed her way through the net until enough strands parted to shake it off the boat, which was almost swamped. *A fishing net,* Alice assumed as she began to bail in earnest, *probably left behind by some trawler.* But it was not a fishing net.

Under the early morning sun Myron barely managed to struggle around the southern tip to the lee of the island. The sea behind him was a turbid madhouse, but here he found things placid. Finally Myron pulled up to a dock, and the red panda leapt out, glad to be on dry land again. As she prowled around the dock, sniffing, Myron clambered awkwardly out of the boat, his legs stiff and almost deadened. He lay on the boards, unwilling, it seems, now that he had come all this way, to leave the shore and trek across the island to find the red shack. The boat, unmoored, drifted away across the glassy water. By the time Alice noticed, it had gone too far to wade after, and Myron seemed unconcerned. Perhaps he had read my *Boy's Life of Cortes,* which tells how the conquistador, after the disastrous retreat of his first invasion, burned the ships of his second expeditionary force on the Mexican coast, to drive home the point that this time there would be no retreat available. Or perhaps he was just in a hurry. He was running a little late.

Myron and the little red panda scrambled inland across a desert of low bushes and cacti. There were no trees to be seen, although in a few places the stumps of petrified tree trunks rose several feet from their calcite roots in the sand. The ground sloped uphill, and the rocks and sand were loose enough to make climbing difficult. Tediously, wet and weary, Myron trudged up the long slope toward the far cliffs, the red panda at his heels. A family of dwarf gray foxes came scuttling out from under a withered shrub to sniff at Alice and scampered away to yip from a distance. And, then, once they reached the long flat ridge of the island's east cliffs, the wind proved stronger even than it had been, and far less predictable. They had hardly been there a minute, resting at the top after their miles of ascent, when a stray gust coming unchivalrously from behind knocked Myron flat over. When he picked his face up out of the rocky ground, he saw that the red panda was caught in the wind, which had lifted her up and blown her out to sea.

For a moment she turned human, in an attempt to gain enough mass to set herself down, but it was too late, she was over the edge, and, as a human, she dropped like a rock.

Myron could only watch, helpless. The wind was too strong for him safely to get close enough to the edge to look over. Who can blame him if he assumed Alice was gone? The wind just kept blowing, bringing with it that haunting whistling it makes, and the unmistakable sea smell of fish and salt.

But Alice—Alice was luckier than she will ever admit. The cliffs were not as high here as they were farther up, but it was still a good two hundred feet down; she turned back into a red panda partway through, though, and was light enough to be bobbled up and down by the wind before she landed in the water. And here the wild sea did not immediately toss her far away, or buffet her to a jelly against the cliff face. Rather, she found herself tangled in a net, a net that had itself been tangled in the rocks, its loose end flopping about in the waves. Being caught thus was awkward in some ways, and encouraged swallowing a lot of salt water, but it did offer a way for the red panda to scurry to the cliffs. Here she tested the rough, uneven surface for pawholds. And slowly, her body hampered by several pounds of extra water weight in her tail alone, she began to climb.

No one saw him, meanwhile, but we can assume that Myron turned south here and headed downhill along the ridge, hoping to see a red shack. He had spent the last two months largely alone, so perhaps he was used to it, but Alice can be charming company, so perhaps she was missed. Perhaps he still missed me. As he walked, he kept his body low, and his feet spread wide for balance. At least that's what he was doing when Alice caught sight of him again. She had worked her way up the cliff—perhaps she exaggerated how difficult it was—and tracked Myron by scent. She tried to keep out of the wind, which slowed her somewhat, but she was gaining on Myron, and indeed she had a visual on him. He was walking in the distance, that peculiar squatting walk in the wind, right up to a red shack. The red shack shuddered as the wind hit it, barely keeping together. A long, charred, lightning rod extended up from its side, vibrating with every new gust. The shack looked newly built and shoddy, and tumbling out of it, like clowns from a car, came a hippopotamus, a wildebeest, an ermine, even, and a man dressed nattily in a white suit. A scar ran across his dark face, over one absent eye and the bridge of his nose. He was grinning broadly.

Myron was gaping at the menagerie, and the man and the scar.

Alice could sense them now, and very sensibly she backtracked and took shelter behind a rock. The wind carried tantalizing fragments of their conversation to her sharp ears, but some parts, I must admit, remain speculative. Certainly the man, noticing that Myron was staring at his scar, said, "Don't worry, boy. You didn't do this to me. The tiger did."

"You're Mr. B—Mr. Lynch," Myron stammered.

The animals arranged themselves in a half circle around Myron. He found himself stepping backwards, closer to the cliff's edge. The hippopotamus, in negotiating for the best space, hit the rickety shack with his posterior, and its walls collapsed into timbers. The inside, it could be seen now, was glittering with a wallpapering of tinfoil.

Marcus Lynch smoothed his sparse mustache. The sun was directly behind Myron, so Marcus had to squint his good eye when he looked at him. He looked like—the cat who had eaten the canary is perhaps an unfortunate cliché, but certainly it applied. "The Rosicrucians told me to build a shack on a certain place, paint it red, and at eight in the morning you'd come to me. You're a little late, by the way. What did they tell you?"

"To look—to look for the red shack. I had to go around the island and back, so I wouldn't miss it. It was farther south than I'd thought. The directions weren't very specific." Myron took another step toward the edge.

"Well, mine were very precise. You should be more careful, Myron, of whom you trust; you have been betrayed. Oh, and surely you don't think you can thwart me this way again," Marcus said. He was really enjoying himself. "Look over the edge, you'll see Benson in a boat. He's spent the last fifteen hours laying nets out, which has been very difficult because of the wind and the waves last night, and because the water is particularly deep just there. But as you can see, after wasting far too many nets, he has finally got the area below covered. If you leap off, you'll find yourself tangled in them, and he will draw you out and kill you."

"Benson left you, he was working for Mignon Emanuel," Myron said.

"I know," said Marcus. "That's why he's down there, doing the wet work, while we stayed up here high and dry." The lion, of course, hated water.

The animals laughed sycophantically at the thought of Benson's discomfort. Their laughs, though, were terrible animal grunts and squeals. The hippopotamus's laugh was especially bad. You will probably never hear a hippopotamus laugh, but, if you ever have the chance to, don't. And then Marcus raised his hand, and the animals all took a step forward.

Myron had risked a glance over the cliff. It was much lower here, probably under a hundred feet, but still a dizzying height. He could see Benson below in a small boat in the center of a sea of nets like a spider waiting in its web. "What do you want from me?" Myron said, turning his attention back.

"Mignon Emanuel wanted to use you as a false messiah, to rally suckers around. The gorilla wanted to use you as an insideman. My desires are far simpler. I want to kill you and see if you really are a wooly mammoth the way some people say. Then I will skin you, sew up your skin with sawdust, and put it on display at my coronation."

From the windswept caves of the cliff below came the echoed cawing of sheltering seagulls. It all sounded so familiar.

"Aren't you afraid," Myron tried, "that I will turn into a mammoth and kill all of you?"

"It is unlikely you know how to turn into anything, but

even if you managed, lion plus hippo plus ermine plus wildebeest can easily defeat a mammoth. The ermine will crawl up inside the trunk, we have the plan all worked out, and it is quite a brutal death. I've been studying your moves, Myron, and I have carefully neutralized all your tricks. You can't leap to safety. Your eldritch words of power have no effect on anyone as old as we. There is no doomsday device to be seen. No cavalry will come to the rescue; the navy is hidden below the ground, and your red panda behind the rocks over there will meet her death once we are done with you."

Alice heard that part, all right. She was probably missing the pistol, left behind in her pickup, sixty-five miles away.

"I suppose I should thank you, really, for removing Mignon Emanuel from the board," he continued. "She was the only one I considered a true rival. My resources are great enough now, with my ermine and all, that eliminating Evelyn should be child's play, once I get rid of this *last loose end*. The embarrassment of *the one that got away*. These phrases describe you, Myron."

At a signal they all stepped forward again. Myron could only take a microstep backwards. He could feel the soft volcanic rock crumbling beneath his foot. He was out of tricks.

The ermine twitched its black-tipped tail in anticipation of blood. Myron recognized the feeling of him from Chicago.

"Did it ever occur to you that I might be the chosen one?" Myron asked.

"Surely, Myron, not even you are naïve enough to believe Mignon Emanuel's confidence games."

Myron sighed. "You know, the first time I stared down my own death, I was really scared. The second time I cried. But by now, it's just something that happens to me. I guess I just don't—wait a minute."

Marcus looked like he had quite been enjoying the speech. "Wait a minute? Why, what's wrong?"

"I just remembered something," Myron said. "I should have thought of this days ago." And he leapt off the cliff. There was a clap of thunder.

"Damn him!" Marcus cried, and after a moment's hesitation raced to the edge to peer over. He wanted to make sure, doubtless, that Benson had netted the troublesome boy and was dragging him into a position where he could somehow turn into a bison and gore him. But when he looked down all he saw was bubbling water and the shredded remains of a few nets. Benson and his boat were nowhere to be seen.

The hippopotamus and the wildebeest, now in human form, ran forward to scan the water for any sign of Myron. And so they all saw the water boil; and there, breaking the water, was the most enormous whale. It rocketed up from the depths, drawing almost its full length out of the water until it stood on its tail. One eye of its huge pointed head was level for a moment with the cliff, with Marcus Lynch and his cronies. The scars were tiny along its enormous face. And then the head twitched to one side; its tonnage came down upon the startled creatures, squashing them flat. Marcus's white suit ripped where a lion's mass, pulped and boneless, burst out of it. And then the whole side of the cliff cracked, and cracked off, and the corpses fell to the sea below, the bulk of the whale crashing in an enormous upthrust of water beside it.

For a moment, the whale circled around in the deep water at the base of the cliff. Then it rose, and from its blowhole it fired one last salute. Perhaps that meant *good luck* among whales. And then off into the boundless ocean it disappeared.

The ermine had managed to slip away, but Alice tracked him through the low scrub and took care of him, too. And then she waited for the windstorm to end, so the navy would come above ground, and she could as a human feign shipwreck survivor and hitch a ride back to the mainland.

And that was the last we saw of Myron. I interviewed several seamen in the days after the storm, and many reported seeing an enormous whale, which some called a blue and some a sperm. One mariner, pleased with his own eloquence, called what he saw "the Moby Dick of whales"; but he was an idiot. Certainly they saw something huge, and then they stopped seeing it, as it made its way back to the deeps.

Years have passed, and years will pass, endlessly and eternally. Evelyn has vowed to bring some sort of order to the jungle, and has even gone so far as to put out a ban on murder. Gloria predictably is calling in response for assassination and keeps blowing her face off trying to make a pipe bomb with pushpins in it; once she masters the theory, she will fill the finished product, she vows, with her nail clippings. After putting it off for far too long, in my opinion, Alice fed a line to the tearful and confused Dr. and Mrs. Horowitz. And I still come down to the shores of both coasts, alternately every few months, and throw bottles into the sea. Sometimes jars, with paperback books I wrote in better days jammed inside, but sometimes just bottles with a curl of paper in each. Gloria calls it bourgeois sentimental and Alice calls it cruel, but all it says is:

Myron.—Wish you were here.

Dramatis Animalia

Ailurus fulgens (Alice): *Do not listen* to what Alice says about *anything*

Alces alces (Spenser): Former legionnaire, former survivalist; mainly a cynic

Arctictis binturong (Arthur Hong): Your humble narrator

Bison bison (Benson): Head flunky; smart enough to know when he's not smart enough

Canis latrans (Angel Sanchez): Sorry about the car, chum

Connochaetes taurinus: Flunky

Gorilla gorilla (Gloria): Anarchist; in related news, kind of self-destructive

Gulo gulo (Svipdag): Not even a proper cameo, really, but still a fan favorite

Hippopotamus amphibius: Flunky

Lemur catta (Florence): Last survivor of a dying race; shorter than me

Loxodonta africana (Evelyn): Not a bad sort, all things considered

Macaca sylvanus (Charles DeRudio): Assassin (failed); cavalry officer

Microtus californicus: In the employ of the Nine Unknown Men

Mustela erminea: Flunky; notoriously shifty

Panthera leo (Marcus Lynch): Nature's deadliest hunter; a bit of a reprobate, really

Panthera tigris (Bima): The second deadliest, it turns out

Pteromys volans: Assassinated Friedrich Nietzsche (?)

Pteropus scapulatus (Allambee): Not really trustworthy; did he mention he's from Australia?

Ursus arctos (Mignon Emanuel): Despot of the Fortress of the Id